Southern Sunrise

SPECIAL EDITION

NATASHA MADISON

Cover Design: Jay Aheer https://www.simplydefinedart.com/

Editing done by Jenny Sims Editing4Indies

Proofing Julie Deaton by Deaton Author Services https://www.facebook.
com/jdproofs/

To Jan who just dropped the little crumb to make this book a reality!

One

ETHAN

"Class dismissed," the teacher says, and I'm the first one out of my seat and out the door. The bright sunshine causes me to squint as I jog down the steps of the campus building. I'm on the way to my truck when the phone rings in my pocket.

Taking it out, I smile when I see it's Emily. "Hello, Sunrise." I greet her with the nickname I gave her when she was fourteen, and we stayed out all night. Her parents didn't know and neither did mine. We watched the stars all night long, and when the sunrise finally came, she looked at me with sleepy eyes, and said, "Hello, Sunrise." It was the day she turned fifteen, and I finally kissed her. We've been together for almost five years. We grew together in a small town, and she is two years younger than me, which is why I waited until she was fifteen to kiss her. But the minute I kissed her, I knew she was the one.

I want to say that it started gradually with the two of us hanging out together, but no one knew we spent every single day together by the creek. One day, I saw her sitting in the middle of a rock at the creek, just watching the water. We got to talking, and well, the rest is history. It started with us meeting "by accident" in town at the diner, and then it got to be where there was no Ethan without Emily by his side. It's why I chose to go to college only an hour and a half away. I couldn't leave her, and it's why I go back to see her four times a week.

"Hey there, Birthday Boy!" she squeals. "Happy Birthday! Am I the first one?"

"Considering where I was with you at midnight"—I laugh—"you were the first one."

She laughs. "Oh, good. What time are you coming into town?"

"My last class just finished, and at this time of day, it takes about two hours to get back to town." I look around at all the people on the campus lawn. It's usually crowded on bright, sunny days because people want to get out.

"Okay, perfect," she says. "Are we going straight to your mom's place?"

"Yeah," I say, stopping in the middle of the huge lawn when I feel as though I'm being followed. I turn around, looking to see if someone is watching me, but no one stands out. "I also figured tonight would be a good time to tell them the big news."

"But it's your birthday," she says. "I don't want to take the spotlight off you." And this is another reason I love her. She is selfless in every sense of the word and puts everyone else's needs in front of hers.

"Trust me, my mother is going to be over the moon with the news that we are getting married," I say, smiling as I think of her wearing my ring. "Just don't forget to wear the ring."

"I told you I don't wear it in case someone sees me," she huffs out. "Anyway, I have to go. Class is starting, so I'll meet you at your mom's place. Love you," she says, hanging up, and my chest feels full when she says this. I look down at the screen saver of the two of us, taken after I asked her to marry me. Her face was still stained with tears while I kissed her.

"Excuse me?" I turn around when a man's voice interrupts my memories. "Are you Ethan McIntyre?"

"I am," I say to the man, looking him up and down. He doesn't look like he fits here, that's for sure. His beard is almost white, and his three-piece suit clearly tailored. "How can I help you?"

He shakes his head, and it's then I realize he's holding a manila envelope. "You can't help me with anything." He looks down at his hands and then looks back up at me. "But I can help you." He extends his hand to me. "This is for you."

My hand moves to grab it before my brain registers. "What is this?"

"Your truth," he says, and just like that, he turns and walks away. Leaving me confused, I call out to him again, but he doesn't turn around. When I look down at the envelope in my hand, I see my name written on the front. When I look back up, he's already disappeared in the crowd.

Opening the envelope, I pull out the papers and start reading. The letter is addressed with just my name. As my eyes scan the papers, I feel like my head is spinning around in a circle. It's almost as if my life is spiraling out of control, and all I can do is watch. My heart speeds up so fast in my chest that I hear the thumping in my ears. I flip the pages over and then come back and read it again. This can't be happening; this is not happening. My legs give out on me, and I sit on the grass. If anyone walks past me, it just looks like I'm sitting down reading papers when, in reality, my life and the foundation I grew up on is crumbling to the ground. I read the paper maybe seven times before I have the energy to get up.

I walk to my truck, and only when I'm behind the wheel do I let the anger rage out of me. I punch the steering wheel until my knuckles are bloody. My body is numb, my mind all over the place with the questions I want to ask and the answers I need to know as I start the truck. The tears just leak down my face as I make my way home.

Home. I laugh bitterly. What the fuck does that word even mean? Do I have a home? Where do I belong? I ignore the ringing of the phone on the passenger seat beside me. It sits right on the papers that have just destroyed my life.

Pulling up to the house, I don't know what's going on inside. I grab the papers in my hand, gripping them so hard the cuts on my knuckles open again and some blood drips out. I walk up the steps that I called home since Uncle Beau and Mom got married. With every step I take, I feel my feet get heavier and heavier.

Opening the door, I hear the hush of whispers. I forgot they were going to surprise me. I walk into the room, and Uncle Beau spots me right away. I look at him, and anger just rips through me. My chest starts to heave as though I've run a marathon.

"He's not my father?" I point at Jacob who I thought was my father. I look at the four people who I trusted with my life —Jacob, Kallie, Beau, and Mom—but none of them say anything, so I ask them again, this time my voice getting higher. "He's not my father?"

My mother looks at me with tears rolling down her cheeks. "It's a lie," I tell them and finally look around to see that most of the town has come out to celebrate my birthday, but I don't care. "It's all been a fucking lie." The words cut me as I say them.

"Ethan." My mother is the first one to say something. "Let's go somewhere and we can talk."

I laugh now, but no one is actually laughing, and my chest hurts. "So what, we can bury the truth some more?" I yell.

"Ethan." Beau says my name, and I turn to him. "I think you need to calm down."

"Uncle Beau," I say. "Well, at least that part is true, right?"

I then look at my father. "You took the fall for someone else." I shake my head. "Why? Why would you do that?" I ask, and all of it clicks into place. "You lost Kallie because of this. When I'm not even your son."

"You might not have my blood running through your veins, but you are mine," he says loudly and through clenched teeth.

"I am not yours!" I scream as the tears fall. "My whole life has been a lie."

"No," my mother sobs out. "Nothing was a lie. You grew up surrounded by love," she says, opening her arms to motion to all the people who stand around, most of them in shock. "It doesn't matter what your DNA is."

"Of course, you would say that," I say. "You had the chance to tell me the truth my whole life," I say. "You had the choice to tell me the truth, and all you did was lie to my face. Every single time you said you loved me, it was a lie." I look around the room. "Take it in, people, take it all in. Ethan McIntyre is not even a McIntyre. I'm a Huntington."

"Ethan, that is enough." Beau steps forward, trying to touch me, but I move out of his reach.

"Why is it enough?" I ask, shaking my head. "You know what is enough? Enough with all the lies and secrets. Enough with pretending that I'm one person when at the end of the day I am no one." I turn and walk away.

"You." I point at my mother. "You destroyed me." She gasps out and falls, but Beau catches her. "I never want to see or hear from you again. It's over." I walk out of the house to the sounds of sobs and crying echoing, and I make it far enough before I feel a hand on my arm.

"Don't you walk away from me, son," my father says.

"I'm not your son," I say. "You are nothing to me. Just like her." I point at my mother, who's now standing on the porch.

I get behind the wheel and peel away from the house. Someone shouts my name, but I block it out. I block everything out, even when the phone rings on the seat, and it's Emilycalling. *She deserves better*, I think to myself. She deserves to have a man who knows who he is. So I do the only thing I can do. I roll down the window and toss the phone as I drive out of town, never once looking back.

Two

ETHAN
FIVE YEARS LATER

A beeping sound gets louder and louder, and then I hear voices. I try to open my eyes, but the pain rips through me. I groan, not sure whether they will hear me, but I do it anyway.

"I think he's waking up," someone says, and I try to move my hands to give them a signal. "He moved his finger." I take a deep breath and concentrate on opening my eyes. The bright light feels as if someone stabbed me in the eye, so I slam them shut again.

"Hello, Mr. Smith." I hear them call my name. I try to open my eyes again, only to cringe and close them again.

"Light," I say, trying to talk, but there is a tube down my throat.

"You have been intubated, Lt. Smith. Don't try to talk," she says, and I want to rip the tube out of my throat. "We are going to take the tube out," she says, and my eyes stay closed while I feel the tube down my throat being taken out. I inhale deeply and cough.

"Get him some water." I hear the door open and then close. "I'm going to close the blinds." My senses take over as I picture someone walking to the window, and I count their steps to see how big the room is. The blinds are closing, and then I hear her voice again. "Okay, you can open your eyes now."

I open one eye just a sliver this time and find the room almost dark. The light from the machines gives off a soft glow, and light from the hallway streams in from the three windows I'm facing. Before I say anything to her, I look around just in case I need to prepare myself. The machines are all behind me, and I spot an IV in my arm. Finally, I look at the doctor with blond hair piled high on her head, wearing a doctor's lab coat with a stethoscope slung around her neck.

"Hi, I'm Dr. Mallard," she says softly, "and you're in Germany." She answers my next question. "You're lucky to be alive, Lt. Smith." Closing my eyes, I try not to think of everyone I left behind. "You were captured for close to fifteen days." She's obviously done this before. "And you were rescued last week." My memories are coming back full force, and I cringe. "You made it all the way here and then went into cardiac arrest. You also flatlined on the table," she says, and I look at her. "Twice. You had internal bleeding, not to mention a ruptured spleen."

The door opens, and the nurse comes in with a plastic glass in her hand with a white straw. "Take little sips," she says gently, and the cool liquid burns all the way down. "Just little sips."

"How long was I out for?" I ask, my voice harsh.

"We had to place you in a medically induced coma for the past two days." She smiles. "I'm happy to say that after some physical therapy, you should make a complete recovery."

"Good to know," I say, closing my eyes again, my body suddenly feeling drained. "How many?"

I open my eyes, looking at her. "How many of us survived?"

I look to see if she has any reaction, and just as I realized before, she's done this way too many times because nothing prepares me for her answer. Even if I knew deep down in my heart that I was the only one, hearing it is a totally separate thing. "You're the only one." I nod at her, not saying another word. I'll blame it on the burning in my throat, but in reality, it's the lump in my throat. I served beside these men who were my brothers, and I would have died for them just as they died for me. "Your commander will be coming by in the morning. Get some rest, Lt. Smith."

The first thing I did when I ran away five years ago was enlist in the military, and the second was to request a name change. I didn't want anything to do with McIntyre or Huntington as my last name, so six weeks after I entered the military, I had my name changed to Ethan Smith. It was also the same day my heart turned to stone.

I glance down at the cuts starting to heal on my arms. Looking at my hands, I see the nails that broke while I tried to claw my way to freedom. I close my eyes and hear the voices again.

"*We've been compromised.*" It was the last thing I heard before a bomb exploded right beside us.

When I open my eyes again, I see that I'm safe and in a hospital room. Ripping the cover off my legs, I look down to make sure both limbs are there. I move my toes first and then bend my knees. Then I try to move to a sitting position, but my body screams out, making me stop. When I look down, I see blood starting to soak through the hospital gown. I hiss out when I move, and this time, I feel the blood dripping. I press the button beside me, and the nurse comes in. "Lt. Smith?"

"I'm bleeding," I say. She looks down, lifting the gown, and I see dark purple welts and where the blood has now soaked through the gauze over the wound. "That doesn't look

9

good," I joke. She just looks down at me over the eyeglasses propped on the end of her nose.

"Should I even ask how this happened?" She reminds me of my grandmother, Cristine, straight and to the point. I shake my head, erasing it from my memory.

"I was trying to see if I had both my legs, and if they worked," I say, and she shakes her head.

"You guys. I'm surprised you didn't try to get off to make sure that worked, too." I laugh now but then look down.

"It'll work," I say, "right?" She laughs, walking over to grab a pair of gloves and new gauze to change the bandage.

"All fixed," she says. "You're lucky the stitches didn't break open." She tosses the gloves and the bloody gauze into the garbage. "Why don't you do yourself a favor and get some rest?" She takes off her glasses. "And please don't try to see if your other member works."

I laugh as she walks out, and I watch her go to the nurses' station. She gets my clipboard and starts writing notes. I fight sleep as much as I can, but when it becomes too much, I close my eyes. My training kicks in, and I relax my body, but my ears stay alert, and I hear footsteps. I wait to see if the steps get closer, and when they stop right in front of my bed, I open my eyes, but nothing could prepare me for who is there.

"What are you doing here?" I ask.

"Came to give you a ride home," he says. I just look at him because I don't know that I've ever seen him dressed in a suit. He stands with both hands tucked into his pants pockets.

"How did you know where I was?" I ask, and he smiles.

"You should know by now, Ethan, that I knew where you were the second you enlisted," he says with all the cockiness Casey can. He looks just the same as he did the day I took off except he now has a bit of white in his hair. I wonder how Olivia is, and the feeling of longing fills me. I shut it down before I start to wonder about the other person I left behind.

"Good for you," I say, the chip on my shoulder bigger than it's ever been. "Now, you can forget you saw me and fuck off."

"Big words for a big man," he says, not even flinching at my words. "You finished with your tantrum?"

"You finished talking?" I counter.

"You almost lost your life," he says, his voice getting tight. "Doesn't that make you see?"

"The only thing it makes me see is the next time I have to be more cautious," I tell him. "Did you tell anyone?"

"No," he says. "It's not my place to tell them. But your mother, she isn't -"

"I don't care," I say, stopping him from talking, my heart in my throat when I think of the last time I saw her. I regretted that moment more than anything in my whole life. But what's done is done, and there is no going back. "No regrets" is my new motto.

"It's time you come home and face the music, Ethan," he says. "If not for you, then for your family."

"I don't have a family!" I shout, and the hurt is even more than it was five years ago. "The only family I did have died right beside me on the battlefield."

"You know deep in your heart that isn't true." His voice stays low. "You know that."

"I know nothing," I say. "And what I do know is that for my whole life, I was lied to and made to believe something that wasn't even true." I sit up, ignoring the stinging of the wound and the fact it's probably opened and bleeding again. "That is what I know." He shakes his head and doesn't say anything. Instead, he walks over to the side of the bed, and I see him take something out of his pocket. I wonder if he's going to show me a picture of my mom and my dad. Or maybe he's going to show me how much Chelsea has grown. Instead, he places a key right beside my hand. "What is this?"

"That is the only time I'm going to extend the olive branch," he starts to tell me. "I promised that I wouldn't say anything to you." I want to ask who he promised this to. "I said I would just come and make sure you're okay. See it with my own eyes instead of hearing it from someone else. I wanted to make sure if anything happened to you, I would be the one telling your parents and not that they bury you with no one knowing."

"They would bury me with my brothers," I tell him.

"You can change your name fifteen times, but at the end of the day, you are still Ethan McIntyre." He turns around and starts to walk out of the room.

"Ethan McIntyre died five years ago," I tell him, and he looks back at me.

"See you soon, Ethan," he tells me.

He doesn't wait for me to answer. Instead, I watch him walk out of the room and past the nurses' station. I wait until I know he's gone before I let the lone tear slip out. I wipe the tear and make my heartrate come back down. "Don't bet on it."

Three

EMILY
FIVE MONTH LATER

"Please note that I'll be giving a pop quiz sometime next week." All the kids groan, and I smile. "Oh, please." I lean back on my desk in front of the whiteboard. "I'm giving you a heads-up, so it's not really a pop quiz."

"Yeah, but then it just has us all nervous," Chelsea says, leaning back in her chair, and I just shake my head. "It's rough, Miss Emily."

"I can imagine how rough it is." I roll my eyes. "You have to spend less time on TikTok and more time reading," I say, and the bell rings. The students get up and gather their things to rush out of the class. It's usually like this during the last class on Friday because everyone is excited about the upcoming weekend. Even me.

"I'm going to study." Chelsea stops in front of me, and I just smile. "Are you still coming over for Sunday brunch?" she asks. I nod my head, and she claps her hands together. "Cool, see you there." She comes in and gives me a hug. "See you Sunday, Miss Emily." She walks out of class, and I walk over to the whiteboard and erase everything, the diamond ring on my finger glistening in the light.

Turning, I sit back down at the desk, gathering the papers and cleaning up for the weekend. Teaching high school students never crossed my mind. When I decided at seventeen that I wanted to be a teacher, I thought kindergarten or maybe second grade. I never thought I had it in me to teach the older kids. But when you get your heart broken, and it's shattered at nineteen, you become so numb that you don't think anything will bother you. I graduated from school ahead of time because I took a full schedule and even went to classes during the summer. I had nothing else to do, and no one else to worry about but myself. I also thought I would escape the town as soon as I graduated, but I just couldn't take that big step. I couldn't move away. A piece of me had to stay in place in case he came back. It was stupid and naïve, and after two years, I finally got it that he was never coming back.

I blink the tears away whenever I think of Ethan and what we had. It obviously meant nothing to him; I obviously meant nothing to him. The promises he made were empty, and I deserved better. It took me a long time to move on, and Ethan would always own a piece of my heart.

A knock on the door makes me look up, and I see Drew. "Hey there, gorgeous." He comes in wearing a blue suit with his blond hair perfectly styled. The smile on his face makes his blue eyes light up. "I was hoping you would still be here."

"Hey, you." I smile and stand as he comes over and kisses my cheek. "This is a nice surprise."

"Yeah, I had a meeting in the area." He puts his hands in his pockets. "So I thought I would swing by and see if you wanted to get an early bite to eat."

"Sure," I say, gathering all my stuff. "How about I meet you at the diner?"

"That sounds good," he says. "Maybe we can do a movie night tonight, and I can make you breakfast in bed."

"Yeah, let's talk about it at the diner," I tell him, not willing to have this conversation in the middle of my workplace. He just nods his head at me and comes in again, kissing my cheek and walking out.

I started dating Drew a year ago, and to be honest, we just fell into it. We used to hang out together with Ethan since they were best friends, and when Ethan cut us both out of his life, we had each other. We started hanging out when he came back home from college to take over his father's insurance company. One thing led to another, and he proposed six months ago. I want to say I said yes because I love him with everything I have, but I didn't. I said yes because he threw me this amazing birthday party and invited all my loved ones and got down on one knee.

No one knows that I stayed up the night before in my hammock, looking up at the stars until sunrise just as I have been doing since I was sixteen. I don't know where Ethan is, and I don't know if he even remembers the date or cares, but deep in my heart, I imagine that he wishes me a happy birthday at sunrise each year. Wherever he is, he looks up, and for that one day, we do the same thing.

After I turn off the light in the room and walk out, I keep my head down, avoiding any eyes. The last thing I want is the town talking about how Drew visited me, and I left with tears in my eyes. I get in my car and make my way over to the diner. I spot Drew outside on his phone as he paces back and forth in front of the diner. He spots me and stops talking, hanging up the phone right away. "Hey." He reaches for my hand.

"Is everything okay?" I ask, pointing at the phone.

"Oh, yeah, just my father," he tells me as we walk into the diner. He holds the door open for me like he always does. I smile at him and walk in, seeing a couple of parents and the kids all wave at us.

"We should have taken it to go," Drew says, guiding us to a booth at the end of the room. "So then you can relax."

"I am relaxed," I tell him, sliding into the booth. "This is fine."

He takes off his jacket and tosses it in the corner of the booth. It should make me want to slide into the booth with him, wrap my hands around his neck, and kiss him. Instead, it just makes me smile. Looking out the window, I wonder what's going on with me. I've been a bit out of it for a couple of weeks now. I don't know how to explain it, but it's like something is coming or something is going to change, and I don't know what it is.

"Are you hungry?" he asks, and I nod. "Me, too."

"I had a granola bar for lunch," I tell him, and his eyes narrow. "I had a meeting with a student, and then I was on duty."

"I told you to start making a lunch," he says. "Or we can finally move in together, and I can make you lunch." I avoid the way he looks at me.

"I told you before," I start to say. "I don't think it's a good idea until we decide where we want to live."

"I think the first step is for you to pick a date." He smirks at me.

"Oh, trust me, I know. Your mother keeps bringing me the bridal and wedding magazines once a month with some of the pages folded down for me to look at." I look around the diner and see how everything has changed in five years. In the beginning, I used to walk in, and everyone would look at me with pity, and the whispers were always the same.

Poor thing is still waiting for him.

Poor thing looks like she hasn't eaten since he left.

Poor thing will never move on. One doesn't forget their first love.

"They want to book the country club," he tells me. "In order to do this, we need to know."

"What if I wanted to get married in the backyard and have a barbecue reception?" I suggest, and he scoffs.

"Honey, you know that my parents want us to have a huge wedding. I'm their only son," he says, and I just nod. We place our orders, and I change the subject to talk about his work.

"I have to go out of town," he says. "My father is hoping to open two more branches in other towns. I might have to be gone for two weeks."

"That's a long time. Will you come home on the weekends?" I ask when the plates are placed in front of us. He grabs his burger and bites into it.

"I was hoping that you would come up to see me." I grab my fork and throw around the salad on my plate.

"It's almost end of the year," I tell him. "I have so much to do to prepare, and then you know I like to give extra help to the students who need it." Something I always wanted when I was a student their age was a teacher who would give her time if she knew I needed help. So, it was a no-brainer once I got my position for the English department.

"You aren't paid to do that," he says, and I feel my blood pressure start to rise. In the beginning, he was supportive and would even offer to come and help. As he got busier at work, he slowly started losing his interest in my teaching as he became more involved in himself.

"I don't get paid to offer extra help in the morning," I say, grabbing a piece of chicken and putting it in my mouth. Suddenly, I just want to leave and put a pizza in the oven at home. "But I do it anyway because if my students are successful and the class average is high, it shows that I'm doing my job."

"Okay, don't get your panties all in a twist," he says to me, and I just shake my head.

I'm about to throw down my fork and walk out of the diner. But that would only get more people talking, so I swallow it down. "What do you say we swing by your house and you grab a bag for the weekend?"

"Um ..." I look at him. "I have a couple of things to do at home." I scramble to think of something in case he asks for specifics. "But how about I come over tomorrow night? We can cook together and then have a movie marathon."

"Or you can just do whatever you need to do next week when I'm not here," he tells me, finishing his meal.

"There is brunch at Billy and Charlotte's house on Sunday," I remind him. It's a weekly thing, but I usually only go a couple of times a month. It's not their fault that Ethan left; it has nothing to do with them.

"Why do we have to go there again?" he asks. "I mean, we went two weeks ago."

I don't tell him the truth because I don't want to hurt him. I go because it's the last piece that I have of Ethan. Being around his mother, his father, his sister, brothers, cousins, it's a piece of him. "Well, if you don't want to come, you don't have to." I grab the glass of water off the table and bring it to my mouth.

"Why don't we just see how we feel on Sunday morning?" he says. "We could always go visit my parents," he says, not giving me a chance to argue. "So are you packing a bag for tonight?" He reaches over the table and puts his hand on mine.

I'm about to break it to him that the only thing I'm doing tonight is going home and slipping into my pjs and maybe eating a pint of ice cream when the door opens. I hear the bell over the door, but nothing, and I mean nothing can prepare me for what comes next. It happens in slow motion, or maybe it's just like that in my head.

The whispers start, and I think I hear a couple of forks

clatter on the table. There are also gasps, and my eyes raise slowly, and my heart stops. After five years, I always imagined the moment he would come back. I also imagined I would be ready for it, but nothing could have prepared me for this moment. His name comes out in a whisper. "Ethan."

Four

ETHAN

I've been pushed to the brink of death. I've made it through all my military training. I've stared into the eyes of evil people. And I've done it without batting an eye or without my heart beating faster.

But this, standing here in the middle of the diner, in the middle of the town that I left five years ago scares the shit out of me. I listen to the whispers I know are going to come, and I even hear a couple of forks clatter. I'm ready for whatever is going to come my way, but what I'm not ready for is to see her this soon after getting to town. My body goes on alert right away when I feel her blue eyes on me. I turn her way, and it is so much worse than I thought it would be. My heart hurts, my stomach roils, and my whole body locks. I don't hear her say my name, but I read her lips. She is just as shocked as everyone is. "Holy shit." I hear and then look at my best friend, who's sitting in front of Emily. "Fucking hell, look who rolled back into town." He shakes his head, and I guess I deserve that. I deserve it all. I left five years ago, and I didn't reach out to anyone. For me, this part of me died when I left.

I nod at him, and I'm about to take a step into the diner

when the door opens behind me, and it's my turn to be stunned. I knew coming back to town was going to shock everyone. I knew that by going to the diner, everyone in town would know. The daisy chain or phone calls would start, and it would get back to everyone that I was back in town. But sometimes, or most times, things never end up like you think they will. This is one of those times.

I turn around, and I'm face-to-face with Chelsea. She's looking down as she walks into the diner, but then she stops and looks up, and her mouth hangs open in shock when she sees me. The shock she feels turns into anger, and I see her eyes flash. "What the fuck are you doing here?" she says, and I look at her.

"Watch your mouth," I say, not thinking that she is now seventeen years old. She looks just like Mom, her black hair is long to her waist, and she has crystal blue eyes. She is so beautiful, and I want to take her in my arms and hug her. I want to tease her like I did when she was younger. I want to put her in a headlock and mess up her hair. Seeing her all grown up just shows me what I've missed.

"You don't get to tell me to watch my mouth," she hisses. I see the huge tears in her eyes, but she is just like Mom as she blinks them away. "You don't get to tell me jack shit. You lost that right." She advances on me, not even caring that I tower over her nor that I can pick her up with one hand. She has no fear in her eyes, none.

"I hate you," she hisses. I'm ready to take her in my arms and let her hate me all she wants. I just don't want to see her crying. But I don't get a chance because Emily has approached and now stands by her side.

My eyes fly to her, and my heart speeds up, just knowing she is within my reach. I take her all in as though I'm memorizing a military operation. She looks the same, maybe a bit thinner but still as beautiful as she was when I first kissed her

21

all those years ago. All I can think about is messing her hair up and seeing if she still tastes like strawberries and still gets shivers when I kiss her right behind the ear. I wonder so many things.

And if seeing her didn't hurt me enough, smelling her and having her so close is like getting kicked in the balls. The hurt and pain are so unimaginable. I was tortured for two weeks one time—I was whipped, beaten, branded, you name it—but this right here is a million times worse.

"He's not worth it," Emily says, the words gutting me. "Just breathe." Chelsea looks over at her, and she blinks as the tears run down her face.

"You have no idea what you did when you left." Chelsea turns around, looking at me. "You have no idea what happened after you left because you didn't fucking care." My heart starts to speed up. "Why don't you do everyone a favor and leave?" She turns and storms out of the diner.

Emily starts to follow her out, but my hand reaches out, grasping her arm. She stops in her tracks, her whole body going tight. She looks at her arm, her eyes fixated on my hand, then she rips her arm away from me and puts her left hand on her arm where my hand was just touching her and it's then I see the rock on her finger. It is almost blinding and so unlike her.

"Don't ever touch me again," she says, her voice low and tight. "Ever," she says and walks out, running after Chelsea. I watch them as Chelsea turns to her and puts her hands on her knees as she has what looks like a panic attack. Her chest rises and falls as she sobs, and Emily rubs her back, bending down to talk to her.

"Hey." I hear from beside me, and see that it's Drew. I turn to look at him, and everyone in the diner is watching our exchange. "You sure do know how to make an entrance."

I shake my head. "That wasn't what I was going for," I tell

him. Drew and I met on the rodeo circuit when we were both ten. We often participated in the same competitions, and one of us would end up getting the ribbon.

"What were you going for?" he asks, and I look at the expensive suit he's wearing and the Rolex on his wrist. "Because I'm not sure you get it." He throws his jacket over his shoulder. "You just aren't welcome here."

"Is that any way to welcome home your best friend?" I ask.

"Our friendship ended the day you fucked off and left us all behind," he says, walking out of the diner. I don't even let a second go by before I'm outside. I watch Drew stand beside Emily and Chelsea.

Chelsea stands up now, and Emily puts her hand around her shoulder and says something to Drew who just nods. Chelsea and Emily turn to walk away, but then Drew calls Emily's name. He walks back to her and kisses her on the lips, and it's my turn to stand here with my mouth open.

You left, I remind myself. You left without looking back. What did you expect? I'm about to take a step forward when I spot a blue Range Rover pull up. The driver door opens, and he takes off his sunglasses.

"I thought they were lying," Casey says. He's dressed more casually in jeans and a T-shirt with boots. What I'm not expecting is for his clone to get out of the passenger side dressed exactly like his father but with a cowboy hat. His dirty jeans and shirt indicate he's been riding. "Quinn," he calls his name. "Go in there and get us a couple of burgers."

"Will do, Pops," he says and then stops in front of me. "You got huge," he says, and then he looks me up and down. "You back for a visit or for good?"

"Haven't decided yet," I say, looking at Casey. "He grew up." I motion to Quinn.

"Well, that's what happens in five years," Casey says,

walking to me and stopping in front of me. "I see you found your way back home."

"Yeah," I say, putting my hands in my back pockets. My stomach feels like there is a roller coaster going up and down in it. "Figured I would."

"You would make things right," he finishes for me. "It's been a couple of months."

"It has." I don't tell him that it took longer for me to recuperate because after he left, I went into a downward spiral. I haven't slept a full night without nightmares since I woke up, and the demons I carry haunt me every waking minute. I don't tell him anything. "I was waiting to get my orders."

"When do you ship out?" He looks over my shoulder at the diner.

"They didn't give me a date yet," I answer honestly.

"Is this the first stop?" he asks, motioning with his chin toward the diner.

"I figured it would get the gossip going," I say. "I didn't know that Chelsea would be here or Emily." I want to ask how long she's been with Drew and why she still stayed if I wasn't here. I want to ask all the questions, but I don't deserve the answers.

The door to the diner opens and closes, and when I look back toward the door, I see that Quinn is coming back with three bags in his hands. "Shall we go check out the house?" he asks, and I nod, but something stops me from walking forward.

"I ..." I look down at my feet. "I should go and see Mom," I say the words that have been lodged in my throat like a lump of coal.

"Ethan," he says softly.

"She is probably going to freak out when Chelsea goes home in that state." I shake my head. "So I might as well get the whole awkward meeting over sooner than later."

I wait for him to say what he wants to say ... to say something. He looks down and then looks up. I can see the tears in his eyes, and I'm not ready for what comes next. I'm not ready for anything he's about to say to me. "I'm sorry, Ethan. She's gone."

Five

EMILY

The sound of her sobs rip through her as soon as I get her in the car and close the door. "What are you going to do with her?" Drew asks, and I have to think that it's the stupidest question he's ever asked me.

"I'm going to take her home," I say. "She can't drive like that. It's not safe."

"This isn't your problem, Em," he says softly. "You aren't even related to her."

"Drew," I say. "I'm going to go take her home. I'm going to make sure she is okay since Savannah and Beau had to go out of town for an event this weekend."

"Then what?" He looks at me, and I want to tell him then I'm going to go home and finish off a bottle of wine. I'm going to call my best friend, and she is going to come over and bring another bottle of wine, and I'm going to finish that one also. I don't tell him that I'll probably be in the middle of the room curled up in a ball and shed all my water weight in tears.

"Then I'm going to go home and grade the papers I need to grade," I say. "I will call you when I get home."

"Fine." He gives in and leans in, kissing me on my lips, no

doubt making sure everyone sees, and by everyone, I mean Ethan. I get into my car and drive away at the same time Ethan walks out of the restaurant.

He's been gone for five years, yet it feels like it was just yesterday. He is much bigger than he was; his arms look massive. His hair is cut short on the sides whereas he had it long before. He used to keep it long because I liked to run my hand through it while we laid side by side on the grass. His eyes are blue, but something about them is different, something I can't explain. It's a coldness, and it's almost scary. "Why is he here?" I hear from beside me. "Why did he just show up?"

"I don't know, honey," I say, my own heart breaking all over again. I thought I was over him, but I was wrong. All the hatred I have for him is there, but so is all the love I felt for him. "Maybe he missed home."

"He broke our family apart," she says. "Mom was a mess when he left. She was there, but a piece of her was gone, and no matter how many times I tried to tell her that he would come back, I would still hear her cry when she thought she was alone. I would hear my dad hold her and tell her that he would be back. He did that. He took that from her, from me, from Keith, and from Toby."

I don't know why I do it. I don't know what possesses me to say what comes out next, but I do it. "He was hurt that he was lied to. He was just hurt. You know how many times you say stuff when you are hurt, but you don't mean it."

"Yeah," Chelsea says, "but after an hour, I'm sorry about it. I don't disappear for five fucking years."

"Chelsea," I say her name sternly. "A lady never swears," I say, and she rolls her eyes.

We pull up to the house, and I see that Keith is just getting home. He throws his bike on the grass, then looks over at us while taking off his helmet. He walks over to us and sees that Chelsea's eyes are all puffy and her nose is red.

"What happened to you?" he says. "Is it that time of the month?"

"Shut up." She pushes him as he laughs and runs up the steps.

"Mom!" he shouts, walking into the house, and I'm shocked she's still there. "Chelsea has her period, and she's crying. Miss Emily had to drive her home."

"I hate him," she says from beside me. The door swings open, and Savannah walks out with a smile. The minute she sees us, her phone rings, and she looks down.

"Mom," Chelsea calls out her name, but she just holds up a hand telling her to hold on.

"Hey, Casey," she says, looking at us, and then her hand goes to the railing. Her legs give out, and she sits on the step. "Where is he?" She listens. "No, I'm home. We canceled." She looks at me with all the tears in the world. "Okay," she whispers, a sob ripping out of her while the phone falls from her hand. Chelsea runs over to her and takes her in her arms as she sits beside her.

"Dad!" she shouts, and Beau comes running out. "Dad!"

"What's the matter?" He runs to his wife and squats down in front of her. "What happened?"

She looks at him with all the love in the world. The two of them have been best friends since they were small and then played cat and mouse until they were forced to get married. She puts her hand on his face. "He's back." Her body shakes with sobs. "He's come home."

Beau looks at her and then looks at me, and all I can do is nod. He looks back at his Savannah and Chelsea.

"I saw him." Chelsea now says something, and Savannah looks at her.

"Was he okay?" she asks, hanging on Chelsea's every word. "Did he look okay? Did he look like he's been hurt?"

"He looks the same," Chelsea says, and I want to tell her that she's wrong. He's different; his arms are bigger. His face is more chiseled; his eyes are darker and hold secrets. He has a couple of scars on his arms, and his hair is shorter. He may look the same, but he's not the same. I look down and blink away the tears that are now threatening to come out.

Savannah looks at me, and she holds out her hand for Beau to help her up. He holds out his hand for her, and she grabs it. She walks over to me with Beau helping her the whole time. If I didn't know she was Ethan's mom, I would think she was his sister. She hasn't aged at all. Sure, her hair has a bit more gray, and her eyes have lost a bit of their spark, but she looks the same as she did in his baby pictures. "He's home," she says to me, and my heart shatters. "He's come home."

Taking a huge breath, I lock my feelings away for at least the next five minutes until I can escape this scene. "I'm happy for you," I say, but my voice cracks, and she grabs my hand. "Happy that he's come home."

"He's back," she tells me, and I look at her.

"I can't go back there," I say, and this time, the tears fall. It's like the dam has been broken. "I can't go back there. I won't survive it."

"But ..." she says, and it's Beau who puts his arm around her shoulder.

"Sweetheart," he says her name softly. "She's moved on."

"I have moved on. I'm engaged to a wonderful man. I'm finally happy," I say, and she looks at me, putting her hand on my cheek.

"Not once did you say you didn't love him," she points out, and I'm about to say something, but she doesn't stop. "A love that deep and that strong doesn't ever go away."

"It was easy enough for him to stop loving me," I remind her, even though the last thing I want to do is shit on Ethan

"He's back, and he's going to explain everything," she says. Shaking my head, I feel arms around me and see that it's Chelsea trying to give me strength.

"There is nothing to explain," I say. "I don't want to hear anything he has to say." I look at Beau. "Nothing he can say will make what he did to me okay." I try not to break down. "He left me. He tossed his cell phone out the window and drove out of town," I say, and she nods. "He didn't see me run after his truck. He didn't hear me yell his name until my voice was so raw I couldn't swallow for two days. He. Didn't. Care."

"Emily," Beau says softly.

"I'm happy your son is back," I say, and then I look at Chelsea, who is wiping away her own tears. "I'm happy your brother is back, but that is where it stops."

"Okay," Savannah says, and then I hear a truck coming. I look over my shoulder and see that it's Casey's blue Range Rover.

I release Savannah's hands when she whispers her son's name. She drops my hand and walks across the lawn toward the car. I watch as Ethan gets out of the truck, and I hear Beau from beside me. "I'll do what I can do," he says softly. "To get her not to bring it up."

"Don't worry about it," I say, turning and walking slowly away at the same time Savannah sobs as Ethan takes her in his arms. She grips on to him, saying his name over and over again as I get in my car. I start the car and drive off, away from the man who broke me, away from the man who shattered my heart, away from the man I thought I hated.

Six

ETHAN

I watch her walk to her car with her head down, and everything in my body and my head is telling me to run after her. But my mother's in my arms, clawing at me, so I focus on her.

Fifteen minutes ago, I stood in front of the diner, and Casey told me she was gone. It cut me off at the knees in more ways than one. I put my hand to my chest to stop the pain from shooting through me, taking a step back.

"What?" I whispered, and for the first time in five years, I had regrets. For the first time in five years, I was brought back to the memory of when I left. I blocked it out, blocked it all out for the last five years, and now I was back there. "When? How?"

"You don't care. At least that's what you said, isn't it?" He looked at me while I glared at him and tried to steady my heart rate. "You wrote them off five years ago, didn't you?" I advanced on him, and he didn't move an inch. He didn't even flinch. "I believe what you said was you had no family."

"I'm not playing with you," I hissed, standing toe-to-toe with him. "Where is she?"

"Dad," Quinn said from beside him.

31

"She's gone for the weekend," he said, and the tightness in my body went away like a huge sigh of relief. "I'll call her now and see where she is." He took his phone out, and he called her right away. "I'll be right over." He hung up. "She's home." I just nodded at him and walked over to the truck, getting into the back. No one said anything as we made our way to the house that I left five years ago.

It had been five years, but it felt like yesterday. My heart sped up as we made our way to the house. Not my house, not my mother's house, not my family's house—just the house. When he turned on the street, if I didn't know any better, I would have thought I was having a panic attack. I reverted to my training, but nothing, nothing could prepare me for the sight before me.

Beau with his arm around my mother's shoulder and her face streaked with tears. She looked the same, but you could see the pain in her eyes. It hit me that I put that pain there. I did that. But I didn't stare at her for too long. Instead, I looked at Chelsea with her arm around Emily, who didn't turn and look at me. My mother saw me first, her eyes meeting mine. She walked to me in a daze, her hand on her mouth as she tried to keep the sob at bay, but it roared out of her.

My body acted in reflex, opening my arms, and she rushed into them. "I'm so sorry," she said over and over again.

Now she's in my arms, and I am watching the car drive away from me. Listening to her tell me she loves me, I remember the times I've been back from deployment when families would meet their soldiers. The tears from both the soldiers and their families usually echo in the big empty room. I would come back and walk right past them to a waiting car.

My head shut off, and my body shut off. I would make my way to my cabin in the woods that I bought and fixed up during the year. It was a shack when I got it—no water, no electricity, nothing—but I fixed it up every single chance I got, and now at least it has the basic necessities.

"You're home," my mother says, pulling out of my arms and putting her hands on my face. "You're home."

I don't answer her. I don't say anything because, to be honest, I have no idea what to say. Am I home? I don't even know what home is. "You look so good," she says, her whole face lighting up, and then she turns to Beau. "Look at him."

"I see him," Beau says with his hands on his hips. He doesn't take his eyes off me, his own tears in his eyes. Chelsea joins him, and he puts his arm around her shoulder as she glares at me. The door opens, and Keith comes out with Toby behind him.

"Is that Ethan?" Keith says my name more of a question. Meanwhile, Toby just walks to Chelsea and grabs her hand.

"Look, guys," my mother says. "Your brother is home."

"Great," Keith says, then looks at Beau. "Can I go to Billy's?"

"Yeah." He nods, and Keith doesn't say anything to me, which surprises my mother. I see the anger in his eyes; it's the same anger I've seen before many times when I looked at myself in the mirror. Whereas Toby's eyes are just confused.

"But your brother is here," my mother says, and I finally speak up.

"It's fine," I say, shaking my head. "I am not going to stay long anyway." Her face falls, and Beau must sense it because he moves forward and puts his hands on her arms. "I just got into town, and I have to check out the place I'm going to stay at."

"What?" she whispers. "You are going to stay here." Her thumb motions to the house. "Your room is exactly the same," she tells me, and I'm shocked that she kept my room. I mean, I wasn't exactly living at home when I left, but I did have my bed and some clothes there. I would have thought that Chelsea would have taken the room since it was bigger than hers. "We didn't touch anything in it."

I'm about to say something to her when I hear a car pull

up, and it stops suddenly. The passenger door opens, and Kallie comes out of the car. Her mouth hangs open, and then the tears come. She leaves the door open as she walks to me. "Oh my god," she says, wrapping her arms around my waist, not giving me the chance. "I can't believe this. I thought they were lying." I hug her with one hand while I look over at the car and see my father get out. Tears fill his eyes but also so much more.

Maybe this was a bad idea, I think to myself. Maybe coming here wasn't the right thing to do. I should have just gone to my cabin and waited for my next orders. I have no idea what to say to my father, so I just go with the basic, "Hey." He just nods at me and stands there with his hands on his hips very much the same as Beau. His look is closed off, and I know it has to do with him being a sheriff and hiding his feelings, but he was the best father you could have asked for, and not once did I ever feel not loved by him.

"Oh my god, you got so big," Kallie says, and I look down at her. She left town when my mother was pregnant with me, thinking my father had cheated on her. Coming back when I was eight, she and my father couldn't fight their pull to each other, and as soon as they ironed things out, she was all in. She came into the house and not once did she not take care of me. Not once did I feel she had any resentment toward me. Not even one time. "Look at how big he is, Jacob." She looks back at him, and all he can do is stand there.

"Yeah." He answers with one word, one little word, and the tension around this reunion is so thick you can cut it with a knife. Everyone's trying to tiptoe around it.

"I have to get home," Casey says. "And I promised that I would get him settled before."

"Oh," Kallie says. "But..."

"I'm not leaving just yet," I say and then look up at my mother who just looks at me.

"You can come to the barbecue on Sunday," Kallie says, smiling, looking around, then looking back at me. "Billy and Charlotte have one every Sunday so we can all get together."

"Um," I start to say. "That sounds good." I look at Casey, who just stares at me. Kallie's arms fall away from me.

"They are going to be so happy to see you," Kallie says. "You know that she is going to be baking and cooking all your favorite things." I swallow down, thinking of how I'm going to face all these people.

I turn and walk back to the truck, getting in while Casey talks to them. Quinn gets into the truck now. "That was rough," he says from the front, looking over his shoulder.

"It was," I answer, the back of my head starting to throb.

"It has been rough," Quinn says. "With Aunt Kallie and Aunt Savannah." My eyes open as I listen to him. "Christmas is the worst. They spend most of the day pretending not to cry, but you can tell." The burning in my stomach comes on now. "And your birthday." I don't have time to answer him because Casey climbs into the car, and we drive away. I try not to look, but for a split second, I look.

Jacob has a shaking Kallie in his arms, and Beau is holding my mother. Chelsea continues to glare at me. "That wasn't bad," Casey says, driving away, and it's Quinn who says something.

"That wasn't bad?" He points back at the scene we just left. "Were you not watching what I was watching? All that was missing is Grandma."

"I mean, it could have been worse?" Casey looks over at him, and Quinn laughs.

"What could have been worse was Chelsea shooting his ass." He points at the back, and I'm shocked she shoots guns.

"She shoots?" I ask, and Quinn looks over at me.

"She's got the best shot out of all of us," he says. "Even me, and I'm older than she is."

I look out the window, my head going around and around, and my eyes suddenly burning. We pull up to the house, and I whistle. "This is new." I look at the one-story house with gray brick stone and a gray roof. The white trim around the windows and the door, and a covered porch in the front with two Adirondack chairs.

"Yeah," Casey says. "We gutted the last one, and well ..."

"Mom went crazy," Quinn says, getting out of the truck, and I see that he's really tall. He's got his mother's model looks, but his father's build. "It was not a good time."

"She didn't go that crazy," Casey says. Only when the door closes, and it's just the two of us does he look over at me. "She went crazy."

I laugh, getting out of the truck and walk over to the trunk getting out my green army bag that holds my clothes. "You joined the Army?" Quinn asks, shocked when he sees me with the bag. "What division?"

"Delta Force," I say, and he just looks at me.

"That is so badass," he says, whistling, and he's about to tell Casey something.

"No," he says. "Your mother would find you on the battle-field and drag your ass home." He shakes his head. "Now wait here while I show him around."

"I don't need you to show me around," I tell Casey, and he just shakes his head, walking up the two steps toward the brown wooden door.

"Everything is wired tight," he says, walking inside and turning on the lights. It's my turn to whistle as I look around.

"He was not kidding. This looks like ..." I look around at the all-white family room that opens to a huge white kitchen with white and gray marble countertops. "I can't stay here," I say, afraid to even dirty the floor. "Why is everything so clean? I'm a military guy, and I'm clean, but all I can see is me drag-ging in the mud."

"Good," he says. "Then I can replace all this shit with normal fucking furniture." He puts his hands on his hips. "If you repeat that to Olivia, I'm going to deny it until my last breath."

"Your secret is safe with me," I say.

"The fridge is stocked, and so is the freezer. TV remote is there." He points to the middle of the table.

"How bad was it?" I look at him, and he just looks at me.

"Bad," he answers. "But it's not my story to tell."

"Did you ever tell them where I was?" I ask.

"Only Beau and Jacob knew," he answers. "I think they shared it, but I never asked."

"Fuck," I say, shaking my head.

"Yeah," Casey says. "That is what we all said. Call me if you have any questions." Casey starts to walk out of the house and then stops. "They don't know about the name change." I close my eyes. "Figured that was your story to tell them." He walks out of the room, and only when I hear the front door slam do I allow my shoulders to slump.

Seven

EMILY

I don't bother wiping the tears from my face as I drive away. I'm on autopilot as I head back to my house. Parking in the driveway, I don't even bother grabbing my bag before I drag my ass into the house. As soon as the door closes behind me and I'm in the safety of my own house, my body gives out.

I collapse against the front door, and my legs give out at the same time the sob rips through me. I lie here in the fetal position as the tears pour out of me, and my body shakes with the sobs that come with it. My eyes remain open, so I can't replay this afternoon and seeing him again over and over in my head.

I hear car doors shut, and then I hear my best friend Jenna start to yell. "She's home. Brett, get my keys in my purse."

I try to move, but I only have enough strength to get away from the door and sit with my back against the wall. I hear the key in the lock and just wait for the door to open. She spots me right away. My best friend since we were seven, and she moved in next door to us. We have been through everything together—first kisses, first periods, and the first time we got caught sneaking out. The first time we decided

38

to do homemade perms that made our hair look like poodles.

"Oh, shit," she says when she spots me. Rushing to me, she squats in front of me and takes my face in her hands. "That fucking piece of ..." she mumbles before I hear Brett behind her.

"She doesn't need this shit." I hear her husband, Brett, behind her. "Move out of the way, darling." The two of them started dating at the same time Ethan and I did. We would go on double dates, but Brett was younger than Ethan, so they didn't have much in common. "I gotcha," he says, leaning down and picking me up like a baby.

"I can walk." I lie to them, and Brett just rolls his eyes. He walks me over to the couch and places me down while Jenna rushes to the kitchen and grabs the bottle of whiskey that I keep on hand.

"I don't think drinking is the right thing to do," Brett says, looking at Jenna. He's six foot five, and she is five foot two. He has blond hair and blue eyes while she has black hair and black eyes. They are complete opposites, yet together they are one.

"Where is Drew?" Brett looks at me.

"He's at his place," I say, and he looks up at the ceiling. "I told him to go."

"I don't care what you told him," Brett says. "How could he just leave you like that?"

"Douchebag," Jenna mumbles. The two of them are like oil and water, and Drew has told me time and time again how he doesn't like her. Jenna, on the other hand, tolerates him just for me.

"I told him to go home." I look at her, trying to defend him.

She slams the bottle of whiskey on the counter. "I don't care if you told him to go home. The point is, you needed him. How could he not see?"

"Jenna," Brett says in a warning tone. "Now is not the time."

"It's never the time." She throws her hands up. "It's now or never, Brett." She looks at me. "Drew is an asshole." I'm about to say something, but she puts up her hand to stop me. "And I know you say you love him, but do you really?"

"Of course I do," I say, but the words don't even sound sincere to me. "He ..."

"He what?" She opens the bottle of whiskey, taking a pull and then hissing. "That's so gross." She points at the bottle. "How do you drink this?"

"I don't drink it," I say. "Billy gave it to me."

"Jesus H," Brett says. "Don't drink anymore of that. It's his special blend."

"What does that mean?" I ask the same time as Jenna.

"It means you are going to get drunker than a skunk if you drink anymore," he says, and Jenna nods her head.

"Good." She walks over to me and sits beside me. "Here, drink up."

"I'm going to go and get food," Brett says. "For later." He turns and walks out of the house. I take the bottle from her and bring it to my lips and take a sip. The amber liquid burns all the way down to my stomach.

"That is so gross," I say. "Maybe it tastes better cold."

"Maybe it tastes better after we're drunk," she says, taking another sip from the bottle. "Still not good."

I put my head down on the side of the cushion. "My heart is broken," I whisper. She's the only one I will tell all my secrets to. The only one I know will keep them locked up.

"I thought I was okay," I say, grabbing the bottle from her and taking a sip as the tears run down my face. "I thought I was over it. I thought, or at least I would tell myself, that seeing him wouldn't matter. It wouldn't change anything. I have so much hatred and anger for him that there is no way I would care if he came back." I close my eyes, and all I can see is him, but it's the new him. The one who didn't smile; the one who I don't know.

"I love Drew." She just looks at me. "I love him, I do ..."

"You will never love Drew like that." Jenna reaches out to hold my hand. "I hate that you can't love him like that even though I think he's a douchebag. I want you to love him with every single beat of your heart. But ..." she says, looking down, and then she has her own tears in her eyes. "You never will. Ethan is the love of your life. He is a part of you."

I bring the bottle to my lips, and this time, I take a bigger gulp. "He was the love of my life, but that part of me is dead."

"That part of you will never die," she says. "Just like if Brett were to leave me. I will forever love him with everything that I have. I will pretend I didn't, but in my soul, I would cry for him."

"He doesn't love me," I say. "If he did, he never would have left me the way he did."

"You need to get the story." She looks at me. "I hate him for what he did, but there has to be a reason."

I shake my head. "What reason?" I ask angrily, getting up. "What fucking reason could there be for leaving me behind if he loved me so much?" I take another sip, and I suddenly feel hot. "He was mad at his parents, and I get that, but me?" I point at myself. "Me? I had nothing to do with that!" I yell. "Nothing," I fume. "He could have reached out after. He could have cooled down and called me. He could have done all of those things." I look at her, stopping to pace. "And what did he do?" She just looks at me with tears in her eyes. "He did nothing. He just tossed me aside without a second thought," I say, and the words hurt my heart even more today than they did before. "I am nothing to him," I say again, and this time, I fall to my knees. "Nothing. How could I love a man who thinks I'm nothing?" My hands go to my face. "How could my heart still love him? How?"

Jenna is beside me as the sobs rip through me over and over again. This time, she holds me in her arms on the floor as the tears flow down and so many tears come. I hurt from losing him just as much today as I did five years ago. For five years, I buried the hurt; for five years, I ignored the hurt. For five years, I pretended that I was okay; I was not okay. I am not okay, but I am going to be okay. "Why?" I whisper. "How could he do that to me?"

"I don't know," she whispers.

"Yeah, I don't either," I say, and when Brett comes back, his hands are full of food.

"So," he says to us. "I ran into Billy, and he said that if you mix that whiskey with some sweet tea, it's even better." He puts down the bag of food. "Also, he says your ass better be at that barbecue on Sunday."

"No way," Jenna says, and I shake my head.

"I don't know how long he's in town for, and I don't care." I get up, leaning on the couch for support. "The only thing I know is that I'm not going to go out of my way to see him. So there will be no more barbecues, and there will be no more lunches with the family." My heart hurts just a touch more. When he left, I got lost in his family; it was the only thing of him I could have so I took hold of it and made it mine. Now I have to step away. "I'm not doing it for him. I'm doing it for me." I walk away from them and toward my bedroom. "I need a shower."

"Do you want us to stay?" Jenna asks, and I look down at the floor.

"No." I close my eyes. "But I'll call you if I do."

"Promise?" she says, and I just nod. I walk to the bedroom and close the door behind me. Taking off the shirt that I put on this morning, I replay the day over and over in my head as the tears fall again. I slip into the shower and the tears mix with the water, and I remember the first time he told me he loved me.

"Sunrise." He called my name while I walked away from him. It was six months after he finally kissed me. We sat by the tree that night and looked at the stars. The sun had just started coming up, so we got up. He held my hand the whole time he walked me home.

"Yeah," I said quietly.

"I love you." He said the words that I'd been secretly telling him every single night. He stopped walking, and I looked at him. I was so head over heels in love with him. "I love you." He cupped my face.

I tried to hide the smile. "Do you now?"

"I do, Sunrise." He leaned forward, and right before he kissed me, he said, "Down to the last beat of my heart."

I get out of the shower and dry off. I avoid looking at myself in the mirror as I slip on pants and a tank top. Walking to the living room, I see that they took the whiskey, but they left food. I walk to the patio door and slide it open, walking into the yard and toward the hammock that I love.

I slip into it as I look up at the stars. The tears don't stop, they don't ever stop, and finally, when I see the pink take over the sky, I get up and go inside, making myself a cup of coffee. Sitting on the back stoop, I watch the sky turn from a pink to a purple. I take a sip of the hot coffee and look off into the distance, seeing a figure walking my way. I just sit here, not sure my eyes are right or if I'm imagining that this is happening. He gets closer and closer, and only when he looks up and sees me does his face fill with shock.

"Emily," he whispers. "What are you doing here?"

"I live here," I say. "This is my house."

"But ..." He looks at the house. "This is my mother's house."

"No." I shake my head, my heart racing like a horse at the derby. "It was her house, and then I bought it from her."

"But," he says, and I look at him. He looks like he hasn't slept either. He wears jeans and a T-shirt that clings to his chest. "But this is ..."

I stand, hoping that my legs don't give out on me. "But nothing. You're trespassing," I say and turn to walk away from him, and he calls my name again.

"Emily." I shake my head and blink away the tears, not wanting him to see them.

"Goodbye, Ethan," I say over my shoulder before walking into the house and locking the door behind me.

Eight

ETHAN

"Goodbye, Ethan." She says the words so softly, and all I can do is watch her walk into the house and listen as the sound of the lock echoes in the air. The last thing I expected was to find her sitting there when I decided to walk here. When I looked up and saw the redness in her eyes, I wanted to take her in my arms and tell her all the things. I wanted to tell her how much I missed her. I wanted to tell her how sorry I was that I left. I wanted to tell her that no matter what happened, I still loved her with every single part of me. I wanted to tell her that I would talk to her at night while I looked up at the stars. I wanted to tell her that I wished she was there every single day. I wanted to tell her that with everything, the one thing I wish I could take back was leaving her.

Do I regret what I said? Yes, in some ways, I do, but it also made me the man I am today. And I'm proud of that man. I'm proud to serve my country. I look around at my childhood home and wonder why the fuck she bought this house. Why did my mother sell it to her when she always said she was going to keep it? I look at the backyard where I spent time kicking a soccer ball. The trees are so big now, and I spot the hammock.

Glancing back at the house, I was thinking back to the time we lay on the grass.

"What kind of house do you want?" I was lying on my back with my hand under my head. Her head lay on my bicep.

"I don't care." She turned to her side. "As long as you're there, and there is a hammock in our yard, we can be anywhere."

She got her house without me, and she got her hammock. I wonder if Drew lives here with her. Fuck, my stomach sinks at the thought. I don't have a right to care. I don't have a right to question her. I lost the right when I left her behind. I walk back to Casey's house even though my heart is pulling me to go back to Emily and get her to talk to me. At least get her to listen to my reason for leaving. I'm almost at the house when I see a horse in the distance, and I would know that horse anywhere. Just looking at her fills my heart as I see Casey riding toward me.

"There you are," he says when he gets close enough. "Was wondering where you went."

Approaching the horse, I reach out my hand. "Hey there, girl," I say, and she backs away from me. "Jesus, even my horse is mad at me."

"Your horse is the least of your issues," Casey says, getting off the horse and handing me the reins as we walk back to his house. "Where did you go?"

"I couldn't sleep." I don't tell him that the nightmares still wake me up, that sometimes I wake up screaming from the pain I endured. I couldn't sleep because I kept seeing Emily in front of me, but every time I would get close to her, she would explode in my mind. I don't tell him anything, but I was awake most of the night.

"Took a walk and ended up back at my old house." His eyes go wide. "Yeah, Emily was outside having coffee."

"Shit," Casey says. He takes his phone out and begins to type.

"Why?" I ask, and he looks up from his phone. "Why is she living there?"

"I'm not going to sugarcoat shit for you," he says. "She didn't do well when you left, and she talked your mother into selling her the house. She wanted to have your home ready for you when you got back." My heart stops in my chest and then sinks to my stomach only to fly back up to my throat. "Your mother didn't want to. At first, she just wanted to give it to her. It was going to be yours anyway when you got married. That's why she kept it."

"She lived in my house." I repeat the words again. "She lived there, waiting for me."

"She did," Casey says. "We told her it wasn't a good idea. Her parents tried to force her not to do it. She ..." He looks down. "She wouldn't listen to anyone. All she kept saying was she needed to make you a home, and you would come back."

"I've been gone for five years," I say. "She's engaged."

"She is," he says, looking out into the distance and then looking back at me. "She deserves to be happy." I want to tell him that she deserves to have a home. She deserves to have it filled with love and to have all the kids she wants. She deserves it all. "I don't want to tell you what to do."

"But you will." I laugh.

"But I will." He looks down. "Dad," he says of Billy, "he had a heart attack a couple of months ago and is resting at home. Mom is hovering over him. If you have a chance, maybe you can go visit them."

I look down. "I don't know," I say. "It's not that I don't want to. It's just ..."

"You fucked up, Ethan," he says, "but the good news is, we won't hold it against you."

"Are you sure about that? Chelsea looked like she wanted

47

to shoot me, and well, Jac-" I can't say his name. "Dad and Beau were there."

"You cut them deep," he says. "You said hurtful things after they spent their whole life trying to make sure you didn't find out. Was it right? I don't know, but it's a decision that they made, and there must have been a reason."

"They lied." I try to say my side, and he holds up his hand.

"I'm not the person you need to have this conversation with," he tells me. "I don't know why you came back or how long you are staying, but ..." He looks out into the field and then looks back at me. "But you need to find peace." He shakes his head. "If not for you, then at least for them."

I don't say anything when he turns and walks away from me toward his blue truck that was dropped off there. "Fuck, what was I thinking?" I ask the horse who just stares at me. "I should have stayed gone."

I wait for the horse to talk to me, but instead, I get on her, and it feels like it was yesterday. I kick her in gear and make my way to the house that helped shape me into the man I am. I see the barn right away and notice that Quinn is on his horse right next to Keith, who just stares at me. I slow down when I get to the barn. "Hey, guys."

"Hey," Quinn says while Keith just stares at me. "I'm surprised she let you ride her," he says of the horse. "She bucks off everyone but my dad."

"Well, I guess I'm special," I say, walking her to the stall I always used to put her in. I look around the barn and notice it's triple the size inside now. "This place is massive." I put her in her stall, get her some water, and then make my way over to the house. I walk up the back steps and hesitate. I'm not sure if I should knock or just walk in like I always did.

I put my hand up, and I'm about to knock when the door swings open, and I come face-to-face with Billy, who looks a little thinner than he did five years ago, but he's still wearing the same old cowboy hat. Tears well up in his eyes when he sees me. "My boy," he says, putting his hands on my face and pulling me to him. This man taught me everything that made me who I am. He taught me to shoot, which is why I'm the best sniper and got into the Delta Force. I was that one percent that was the best in my category. "Glad to see you home," he says, and then I hear another voice from somewhere inside.

"What is all the fuss about?" She comes to the door, wearing her usual apron while she wipes her hands. "Oh my god," she says when she sees me. "Is it really you?" she asks, shoving Billy away from me. "Oh my lord," she says, tears running down her face. "I've prayed for this moment," she says, grabbing my cheeks in her hands and bringing me down to her. "Every single night, I prayed to see you just one more time so I could tell you how much I love you," she says, kissing my cheeks. I wrap my arms around her as she cries. "I can't believe it."

"Grandma!" I hear yelling from the house. "I think the pies are ready."

"Oh!" She pushes away from me. "Don't you dare think about leaving here without eating. You better go wash your hands and get your behind in that chair." She points at the chair, and I see her glaring at me.

I look over at Billy, who wipes tears from his eyes. "I wouldn't mess with her."

"I've been to active war zones," I let slip, and he looks at me with shock, "yet the look she just gave me is scarier."

"You serve our country?" he asks, and I just nod. "Thank you for your service." He comes closer to me. "Just for today, let's not tell her, shall we?"

"Will do." I laugh and look over at him as he just looks at me.

"God, it's good to see your ugly mug," he says in almost a whisper.

"It's good to be home," I say, nodding. "Not sure if it's actually good. So far, it's been far from good."

"You left people behind without looking back. It's not going to be easy." He shakes his head and squeezes my shoulder. "It's a two-way street. Just as much as you were hurt, you hurt the ones you love the most."

"I know," I say. Looking down, I'm not ready to think about it.

"It'll work itself out." He folds his arms over his chest.

"I'm not sure about that," I say, feeling the pressure in my chest.

"It has to. It's how family works." I nod at him. "Now, let's get in there before she loses it again." We walk in the house, and it's almost the same. There are just more family pictures on the walls and scattered around the house. I walk to the kitchen, and I'm shocked that Chelsea is here.

"Hey," I say. She avoids my eyes and looks at Charlotte.

"Is there much more to do, or can I go ride?" she asks, and Charlotte just smiles. "Thanks, Grandma, and I promise I'll be here tomorrow bright and early to help you prepare."

"Last time you did that, you drank some of Grandpa's sweet tea." She puts her hands on her hips. She is so beautiful and sassy, just like Mom. She shrugs her shoulders and walks to Charlotte, giving her a hug. "Love you."

She gives her a hug and walks over to Billy, who whispers something in her ear, and she just laughs. She walks out of the house without saying a word to me. I look at my grandparents and then look at the door. "I'll be right back," I tell them, walking out the door and calling her name. "Chelsea." She ignores me just as I knew she would, and I jog to catch up with her. "I'm talking to you," I say. She turns, and I see the tears running down her face.

"I don't care!" she yells. "Just like you didn't care five years ago."

I swallow down the lump in my throat. "You don't understand."

"You're right, I don't," she says, shaking her head. "I don't know what it's like to have a piece of my mother gone. I don't know what it's like to have to tiptoe around her on your birthday. I don't know what it's like to listen to her cry when she pretends she's okay. I don't understand any of that." She doesn't even give me a chance to say anything before she continues. "I'll never understand how you could just turn your back on your family." She wipes away her tears. "This time, maybe you can say goodbye before you leave us behind again." She turns and runs toward the barn, leaving me to watch as I try to catch my breath.

I watch until she enters the barn, and I know that other people can watch her as I turn back and walk to my grandparents' house. During the whole meal, they tiptoe around asking me any questions. It's almost as though they are afraid to say anything to upset me. My grandmother busies herself in the kitchen, and the whole time, I see her looking over and smiling as she wrings her hands, and when I kiss her goodbye, she has tears in her eyes. "Are you leaving town?" she whispers, and I shake my head.

"Not yet," I say, and she nods.

"Okay, come back and visit." She puts her hand on my cheek.

"He'll be here tomorrow," my grandfather says for me, and I look over at him. "Family barbecue, it'll be a good time for you to catch up and see everyone. Five years is a long time." I just turn and walk out without confirming anything.

I'm walking into the house when I get this feeling that I'm not alone. The hair on the back of my neck stands up as I cautiously make my way into the house. After going room to room to check, I find it empty. I run my hands through my hair and hold my head as my heart rate goes back to normal.

Grabbing my workout gear, I head down to the barn across the yard. I open the doors and shake my head at the state-of-the-art training facility. The walls are covered in mirrors so you can see what you're doing. The middle of the barn has ten weight machines in the shape of a square that works your core. Five bikes on one side of the wall sit right next to five Stairmasters. There are two leg press machines against the other wall with three punching bags and five treadmills. There is an empty space all the way at the end where two ropes lay. If I know my uncle, he had all of this here the minute he gave me the key to the house.

I get on the treadmill first and run until my legs burn. Faster and faster as if I'm running away from the enemy. I work out until my body is about to give up on me and my arms shake when I pick up a weight. The sweat just pours off me, and the muscles in my body fill with blood. I'm sitting on the bench drinking water when I see a shadow enter the barn.

I knew this moment would come. I knew it had to be done. He walks in, his shoulders square, and just looks at me. "You were in the house before?" I ask, and he doesn't say anything. He just stands there in front of me.

"Figured we had a couple of things to talk about," he says. Folding his arms over his chest, he shows me he's ready for whatever I throw at him. For my whole life, I looked up to him, and I wanted to be him. I wanted to be the one who kept people safe. I wanted to be the one people went to when they had a problem, and I would solve it. To me, he was a hero, but he was also the one who lied to me. "That is if you're man enough to stay and actually talk it out and not run away with your tail between your legs."

I laugh. "I didn't run."

"Oh, you didn't?" His eyes glare at me. "What do you call someone who doesn't even stay and find out the 'truth'?" He uses his fingers to make air quotes.

"I call that person someone who needed to find out who he was," I tell him, getting up.

It's his turn to laugh. "Does DNA matter that much to you?" he asks, and I want to tell him it does. I want to tell him that it wasn't his decision to make. "Are you ready?"

"For?" I ask.

"The truth," he tells me. "My part in it, at least." He starts talking before I have time to answer him. "I was going to prom with a ring box in my jacket pocket, and I was going to ask Kallie to be my wife," he says. I've never heard this part of the story. I mean, not that my parents told me much, just that they loved me. "I was so nervous, and I thought I would fuck it up so bad." He shakes his head. "And right before we entered the school, I saw your mother by a tree." He looks down now. "That's not my story to tell in how she got there, but she asked me for help, and there was no turning back."

"She stuck you with someone else's kid!" I shout at him.

"No." He shakes his head. "She didn't make me do anything that I didn't want to do."

"You lost Kallie because of that." I squeeze the water bottle in my hand.

"And I'd do it again and again," he says, but I never wanted to hear those words. I wanted to paint him as the bad guy who lied to me the whole time. "I was angry that I lost my life. I can't say I wasn't, but when the nurse placed you in my arms, something inside me shifted." Tears well in his eyes.

"I had a purpose, and that was you." He looks me straight in the eyes. "It didn't matter that you didn't have my blood; you were mine. I was the one who slept sitting up for four months because you had colic, and your stomach would hurt if you lay down flat. I was the one who held your hand when you tried to take your first step." His words hurt, the anger in them, the hurt in them as he retells my life from his eyes.

"I was the one who dusted you off and made you try again.

53

I was the one who held the back of your bike when you wanted to ride without training wheels at four years old. I was also the one who bandaged you up when you fell off and bruised both your knees. I was the one who held your hand when you walked into school on the first day and who was there when you got mad or sad. I held you when you had nightmares. I was the one who helped make you into the man you are today and the one you came to when you wanted to ask Emily to marry you. I was the one." He points at his chest. "Not some man who shares your DNA. Me." The hurt roars through him. "I'm your father. I don't care what any DNA test says. I'm the one who's fucking loved you unconditionally your whole life."

"Why not tell me?" I whisper.

"What good would that do?" he asks.

"It's better to lie to me?" I ask, my voice getting louder. "You think finding out that you've been lied to your whole life is better?"

"I think making you the man you are was better than a DNA test. I think you are thriving, and having love around you is better than that." He looks at me. "I was wrong. But you leaving and shutting us all out? That ..." he says, his voice going loud. "That's not the man I taught you to be. That isn't the man Beau taught you to be. It sure as fuck wasn't Billy who taught you that."

"I guess I'm like my father, after all." The minute I call the man my father, he takes a step back and puts his hand to his chest as if I shot him. "I didn't ..."

He shakes his head. "Nothing will be good enough for you," he says, his words broken now. The man in front of me who faced whatever danger came his way with his head held high is now slumped over, and I made him hurt like that. "I love you, Ethan, with every single blood cell in my body even if it doesn't match yours. I would die for you because that is what a parent does. I would stand by your side and fight, but that's not good enough for you." I look down at my feet, and the words are stuck in my throat. "I guess we know where you stand."

"And where is that?" I ask, trying to pick a fight with him for no reason.

"I gave you my name," he says, and it's me who blinks away tears. "My father gave you his name because he knew that no matter what, you would be one of us." The tears pour down his face. "But you'd rather erase me from your life. Erase my name from yours. Erase all the memories you have of me and the good times we had. You would rather dwell on that one little thing." He turns around and walks out of the barn with his head down and his shoulders slumped. "I don't know what more you want from me. I came here and gave you my side of it, and that's all I can do. All I ask of you is that you don't treat your mother or Kallie with resentment." He blinks away the tears that I see swimming in his eyes. "They don't deserve any of this," he says. He walks out, leaving me to sit down, and I finally let out the tears I was holding back.

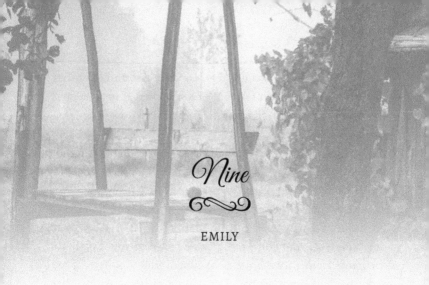

Nine

EMILY

"What do you mean you're leaving today?" I ask Drew as he stands in the middle of my kitchen. After I closed the door and locked it, I dragged my ass to my room and blocked it all out. I slept until I heard a knock on the door, opening it to see Drew standing there in his khakis and a polo shirt.

"I mean that I have to be in town for a meeting tomorrow," he says.

"A meeting on a Sunday?" I ask, confused.

"Yeah, the CEO of the company takes off on Monday, and the only time he could squeeze me in is tomorrow." He leans against the counter. "I couldn't say no. It's a big deal that he's even talking to me. If I land this account, it'll be huge."

"I mean, if you have to go, you have to go," I say, putting the kettle on the stove to make tea. "I'm just ..." I look down. "It's the weekend, and I thought we were going to spend it together."

"Well, how about I make plans for you to join me next weekend?" he suggests, and I just shrug.

"It's just a busy time of year. You know this. It's almost

summer break, so there is so much going on. Not to mention the school carnival," I remind him. "I just can't leave."

"How about we just table it and see how you feel next weekend?" I'm about to tell him that it's going to be the same answer, and he really needs to start listening to me when there is a knock on the door. "You expecting someone?" he asks. My heart picks up, thinking it might be Ethan—that he came back to talk—but I don't tell him that. Walking to the front door, I open it and see that it's Olivia.

"Well, hello there," she says, walking in, and I just take her in. She's the prettiest woman I have ever seen, and I always want to dress and look like her. She just has a sense of style that comes off as not even trying. "I was wondering if you had time today to help me out." I look at her. "I am in the middle of planning the carnival, and I would love some input."

"Oh, of course." I smile at her. "Come in." I turn and walk back to the kitchen. Drew is scrolling on his phone.

"Oh, hello, Drew," Olivia says, putting the paper on the island. "Don't you look handsome."

"Thank you." He smiles at her. "Honey," he says to me, "I'm going to get going, so I can take my time driving there."

"Oh," I say, surprised he's leaving right away. "Okay." I look at Olivia. "I'll just walk him out, so make yourself at home." As we walk down the hallway to the front door, our hands don't even touch. I turn to hug him, and he hugs me with one arm. "Call me when you get in." I smile at him, and he gives me a little peck on the lips.

"Will do," he says, turning and walking out. I watch him leave, waving to him, and then ignore the voices in my head.

You need to let him go.

You don't love him.

You don't want to spend the rest of your life with him.

He deserves to have someone love him with their whole heart and not just a piece of it.

I walk back to the island, trying to get my stomach to settle, and give her a fake smile. "Did you know that I was a number one faker smiler?" she says to me as she makes tea. "I was so good at faking that I was okay that it became a habit."

"I'm fine," I say, slipping onto the stool because my legs are not steady enough to stand.

"I used to be fine also." She looks at me. "Then, I wasn't."

"It's just a bit too much," I finally tell her. She's been so nice to me ever since I started dating Ethan and even beforehand. But when he left, she along with Kallie and Savannah gave me the strength I needed. They held my hand while I cried, while we all cried for him.

"Do you know that I came here to hide?" She begins her story. "I was running away, and this place welcomed me. I have never felt so much love in my whole life." I listen to her in awe as she tells me her story. She gives me all the horrid details, all the scary parts, and all the parts that made her the woman she is. "Love, it isn't easy."

"But it should be," I say. "It's black and white. You either love or you don't."

"Not if someone is lost," she tells me. "Not if someone is fighting himself. Fighting to see them instead of seeing the good."

"I can't do it," I say. "I won't survive it."

"But what if it's different?" she asks. I know now that she didn't come over for the school carnival or because she needed my help. Instead, she came over to hold my hand and make sure I was okay. It's another reason I love the family; to them, I was family. To them, I was one of them, but to them, he was their everything.

"But what if it isn't?" I say. "I can't risk it. I won't risk it. He's back, and I have to make my peace with that," I say, grabbing the tea and bringing the cup to my lips. "We are two adults. We can co-exist."

"Do you think you can actually do that?" I look at her, thinking of my answer.

"I have no idea," I say. "He made his choice five years ago. I get to make my choice now."

"Good," she says. "The best time to meet the bull head-on is to do it wearing red." I laugh, thinking about how she tries to country almost everything. "Tomorrow, he's going to be at the barbecue and so will you."

"Oh, I'm not going to be there," I say. "I'm not doing that."

"Well, I have a message for you." I listen to her as she sips her own tea. "From Billy."

"Oh, dear," I say, putting down the cup of tea.

"If you aren't there tomorrow, he's coming to get you." She smiles. "And from that, you can assume that all of them will follow since he isn't allowed to strain himself."

"Oh, god." Closing my eyes, I know there is no getting out of this. "Fine. I'll call Jenna."

"Good. Now ..." She sits next to me. "Let's go over some things for the carnival."

We spend a good three hours making sure we have everything in place, and when she leaves, I'm really excited about the carnival in two weeks. I make more notes while I watch television, and the loom and gloom of the barbecue hanging over my head means that sleep doesn't come easy.

I finally give up at dawn and get up. Making my coffee, I walk outside and take a seat on the porch to watch the sunrise. When I put the cup in the sink and walk to my bedroom, my stomach is in my throat. My heart is beating so fast that I have to sit several times while I get ready. I've changed at least forty times by the time Jenna yells that she is here and end up sliding on the white shorts that I feel most comfortable in. I roll the hem just a bit, making my long tan legs look even tanner. Grabbing a blue and white striped button-down shirt, I slip it on, then roll the sleeves up to my elbows and tie the front in a knot. I slip on my brown flip-flops, and I'm about to tie my hair when I hear a whistle behind me.

"God, I wish I had your legs," she says, and I shake my head. "You ready?"

"Nope," I say honestly. "Not even close, but we are going to go," I say. "I'm going to smile and laugh, eat good food, and then I'll come home and hopefully not throw up."

"Well, that sounds like a banging time. We should rush over there," she says, making me laugh. "Brett says he is going to meet us there." I don't say anything, and when I get into her truck, and we get there, the barbecue is already bustling. We have to park out onto the road because all the trucks are already there.

"It's crazy how many people come every single weekend," I say when we walk onto the grass and toward the backyard. There are four barbecues every week; the men take turns. I spot the teenagers all the way at the back, trying to play soccer. I make a quick scan of the backyard, and I don't see him. My heart, on the other hand, doesn't care and still picks up speed. "I might have to have one of Billy's sweet teas." I lean over to tell Jenna, and she just laughs.

"Sweet tea, my ass," she says. "That shit made me do things I never thought I would do." She grimaces.

"I don't want to know or for you to tell me," I say as we make our way over to Billy and Charlotte, who are greeting everyone. "Hey there," I say, giving her a big hug and then hugging Billy. "Smells amazing."

"It's nice to have you," Billy says. "Although I was hoping I would have to come and get you, and she would let me out of her sight." He motions to Charlotte with his head, and she wraps her arms around his waist.

"I'll never let you out of my sight." She smiles at him, and he just leans down and kisses her.

"Now that." I point at them. "That's the love you want in your life," I say. Laughing, I turn to walk away and slam into someone. I know right away who it is; my body knows who it is. My heart definitely knows who it is. His hands grab my arms to make sure I don't fall, and my hands go to his hips to steady myself. I swear all the laughing and talking stops as everyone watches this one moment. "I'm sorry," I say to his chest, my eyes never looking up at him. He smells the same; no, he smells better than he did before. My body goes on high alert, and I drop my hands and step out of his reach, walking around him. My gaze never meeting his.

"Holy, fuck me." I hear Jenna mumble next to me. "He's ..."

"An asshole," I finish for her and walk to the table where the drinks are. "Are people still looking?" I ask, and she looks around. "No, but he is."

"Fuck," I mumble and blink away tears. "This was such a bad idea."

"No," Jenna says, grabbing her own sweet tea. "A bad idea would be you not coming."

"This is true," I say and avoid the eyes that I know are staring at me.

Ten

ETHAN

I know it's her the minute I start walking toward my grandparents. I'd know the sound of her laughter anywhere, and then I hear the words that cut me deep. "Now that, that's the love you want in your life."

She turns to walk away from them and runs smack into my chest. My hands reach out to make sure she doesn't fall. Her hands go to my hips, and my whole body goes on alert. I get so tense that I'm afraid I'm going to hurt her arms. The chattering around us stops, and everyone is looking at us. I look down, seeing her face and hoping for one minute that she looks up at me, and I can see her eyes.

"I'm sorry," she mumbles as her hands fall from my waist. She walks away from me, and I can't stop my eyes from following her. Her head stays down until she hits the drink table, and then Jenna turns around to glare at me. I swear if looks could kill, I would be ten feet under already.

"Don't go there," my grandfather says, and I look at him and my grandmother, who blinks away tears. "You don't go there." I look down and then up. "You need to fix yourself before you go there." My grandmother walks away. "There are demons inside you, Ethan. You need to get them out before you take that step."

"She's engaged," I say.

"Doesn't mean shit," he spits. "That man is not good enough for her. The only reason she probably took him was that he was another connection to you."

"Emily wouldn't do that," I say, ready to argue with him.

"Not the same Emily you left behind," my grandfather says, and all I can do is look back at the table. Only, she isn't there. She's hugging my mother and then moving around the yard, saying hello to everyone. She smiles as big as she can, but it's as fake as can be. Not once do her eyes light up when she smiles. Not once do her eyes crinkle at the sides. I watch her from afar the whole time. I say hello to all the people I left behind. I say hello to my cousins, who are now grown. None of them say more than hey to me. Forget about Chelsea, Keith, and Toby—who don't even come my way—and I'm not even going to mention Amelia and Travis, who pretend I don't exist. My mother doesn't leave my side for long, and when she does, it gives me a chance to breathe. I look around, seeing that Jacob is off to the far right with Kallie by his side the whole time as they sit at the table with Casey, Olivia, and Beau. None of them get up or come say hello to me.

"We should get a picture," my mother says to Billy. "All the boys are here. We need a new one for the bar." She calls Quinn over and asks him to go wrangle all the boys, and you can see that he's uncomfortable.

"Why don't we do it another time?" I say, and she looks at me. "All the kids are playing."

She smiles and nods. "I'll be back." Turning, I walk away from the barbecue and make my way to the barn. I look around, seeing if I can spot Emily. I spot Jenna with Brett laughing with another couple. Walking away, I enter the barn, and then I hear her voice.

"You are so pretty," she says. I watch her petting my horse, and it's like she's telling her all her secrets. "Oh, don't you get all feisty on me." She laughs at her as the horse huffs at her. "I snuck two apples and four sugar cubes."

"It's not good to give the horse too much sugar," I say, startling her. She turns to me, and the only true smile she had all day is gone when she sees me. "I didn't know you would be in here."

"I was just leaving." She turns and walks past me.

"Emily." I call her name, and she stops walking, but she doesn't turn around. "We need to talk."

She turns now and looks me straight in the eyes. "Anything you had to say to me ended up on the side of the road when you opened the window and threw me away."

"I didn't throw you away." I advance on her. "I would never."

"Oh, but you did," she says. "Besides, I don't think there is anything you have to say that I want to hear." She wipes away a tear. "Nothing." I let her walk away from me, knowing that here's not the time or the place for this. I let her walk away, knowing that the next time I won't let her walk away from me.

"It took her a long time," my mother says behind me, "to get over you." She walks in now. "It took us a long time."

I look down now, not sure what to say. "Yeah."

"I've been on pins and needles since you got here," she starts, and I see her wringing her hands. "And I know that Beau said to give you some space"—her head shakes as she wipes away tears—"but I just can't."

"We don't have to do this today."

"No, we do," she says. "For my sanity, for the kids, I need to say something." She closes her eyes. "I thought telling Beau would have been hard, but telling you ..." She lets out a huge breath. "I didn't have the best upbringing." She starts her story. "I was pregnant and alone. He told me he loved me, and

I was stupid enough to believe it. Then he hid behind his father and made him deal with me."

I step forward to her. "Please don't. I need to get this all out. I had no one to turn to, and I couldn't tell the one person I wanted to tell. I caught Jacob while he was walking into prom, and I didn't give him a choice. I was the one who didn't want anyone to find out," she tells me. "I was the one who kept it a secret and begged him not to say anything. It was me." She finally sobs out. "You can't hate him for what I did. You were raised surrounded by the best male influences you could ever want. You were raised to be polite and kind. You were raised with morals and compassion, something that Liam didn't have in him. We loved you with everything that we had. We love you with everything that we are," she says. Beau comes running in and takes her in his arms.

"It's okay." He rubs her back. "It's all okay."

"I have to tell him," she says, pushing through.

"To question who your father is after everything he gave up for you." She shakes her head. "You have to know in your heart that he is your father regardless of whose blood runs through you. At the end of the day, you're mine, and you're Jacob's, and I will fight anyone who says otherwise, including you."

She sounds angry now. "I know we lied to you, and I would do it again. But your life wasn't a lie; your life was filled with so much love you wouldn't need to walk because we would carry you. He searched for you the minute you left. He went to Casey, and well, not nice things were said, but he wouldn't let him hide anything. They didn't tell me all the details; they would just tell me you were safe. But ..." She looks down and blocks the sob from her mouth with her hands. "The day you changed your name." My mouth opens. "Casey told him, and he collapsed on his knees as if someone had shot him in the chest. He tried to be strong the whole time, but that day, it took something from him. It took a piece away from him." She shakes her head. "That's what leaving did to the man who gave up everything for you. He didn't give you his blood, but he gave you his name, and to me, that is more than just donating DNA."

"I never meant to hurt you guys," I finally say. "I never meant to hurt you guys. But you have to see that I doubted everything. It made me doubt everything."

"Then we didn't do a good enough job," Beau says, and I want to tell them that they did everything right. "Because if we had done a good enough job, you wouldn't have to doubt who you were or who you are."

"It wasn't that easy," I say, and he shakes his head. He's about to say something else when Keith runs in, calling Beau.

"Dad!" he shouts. "Chelsea is going to take the truck home."

They look at me, not wanting to walk away. "We can finish this at another time," I tell them, and they walk away, leaving me by myself. Walking out of the barn, I avoid everyone this time. Billy sees me, and I just raise my hand, telling him I'm going. I don't look for anyone else, and when I walk up the step to the house, I have to sit down. I feel like I've gone into a battlefield with no protection. My heart is torn into a million pieces. My mind is so scrambled that I have to close my eyes, and when I do that, the only face I see is hers. Her smile and her laughter as she looked at me as though I hung the moon and stars.

It happens so fast that I don't have time to stop myself. I don't have time to think about what it's going to do. I have no time for anything. Because my body is on autopilot, and I have to see her.

I walk toward the house and see that no lights are on in the house. The stars are blinking in the sky, and I stand out here, and I'm about to knock when I hear her from behind me.

"You shouldn't be here," she says, and I turn and see the hammock swinging side to side.

"I ..." I run my hands over my face. "We need to talk."

"We don't need to do anything," she tells me. "The only thing that needs to happen is you need to leave." She walks past me, and I grab her arm, but she rips it from my grasp. "There is nothing you have to say that I want to hear."

"I love you." I repeat the three words that I said to her every single day since I left. She walks to me, and I don't see it coming, but her hand hits my face.

"I hate you," she says, turning and storming up the stairs. The door slams so hard it's a wonder that the windows don't shatter.

"I'm not leaving this time!" I shout, wondering if she even heard me.

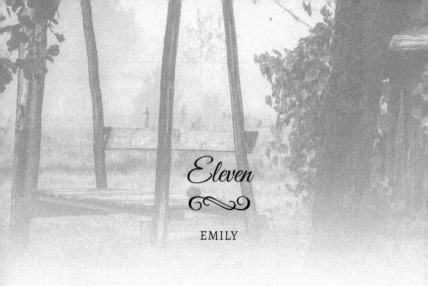

Eleven

EMILY

My hand shakes as I lock the door behind me, and I look down, staring at it. "Stop it." I talk to myself.

"Emily!" I hear his voice as he shouts from the backyard. "Em." When I hear him use my nickname, my hand isn't the only part of me that's shaking. My whole body is shaking now, and I put my back on the door and slowly slide to the floor. The tears fall without me even knowing, the sob comes out silently. "Em." I hear his voice and know he's right on the other side. "Em."

The softness of his voice when he calls me that hurts more than it did when he left. Knowing he's right there behind the door and I can run to him and wrap myself around him.

Closing my eyes, I try to block out his voice, block out all the memories that have suddenly escaped from the locked box I keep in my head.

"Em." He called over to me as I walked away from him after getting mad for I don't even know what.

I turned and looked at him. He stood there with his hands in his pockets. "What do you want, Ethan?"

"For you to come here so I can kiss you." He smirked at me, which made me even madder at that moment.

"No." I shook my head and crossed my arms over my chest. "I don't want to kiss you right now, Ethan."

"What if I come to you?" he asked. I already knew that whatever I was mad about was not even a thought. He took a couple of steps my way. "What if I was the one who came to you?" He took the remainder of the steps until he was right in front of me.

"You made me madder than a wet hen," I told him, and he just laughed as he put his forehead on mine.

"You make me a better person," he whispered. "I'm sorry."

"For what?" I asked, putting my hands on his hips as my fingers held on to the loops of his jeans.

"For whatever made you not smile." He took my face in his hands. "I never want to be the one who makes you frown, Sunrise." His lips touched mine, and I forgot whatever I was mad about.

"Em." He says my name again. "Please. I just need to talk to you. Please hear me out, and then I'll leave." I slowly get up and unlock the door. He sits on the porch in the darkness with his head down, but his head flies up when he sees me. "I wasn't leaving this time," he says when he sees me. "Not this time."

"Ethan." I've whispered his name to myself for the past five years. I used to stand there in the middle of the kitchen and say his name until it didn't hurt anymore. I would say his name in my dreams as I chased him. I would say his name while I curled into a ball and cried out for him. "We don't have to do this." I swallow down, my mouth suddenly dry. "All we have to do is be polite when we see each other, and that is it."

"Sunrise," he says. I walk out of the door with my hands balled by my sides.

"Don't call me that!" I yell. "Let's just get this over with. I have things to do to prepare for tomorrow."

"There are some things that we need to talk about," he says. I stand, folding my hands over my chest to stop them from shaking.

"Really?" I say. "I don't think we actually have anything to talk about."

"You know that isn't the truth." He stands, but I don't want him to come closer to me. I can't do this if he's any closer.

"The only truth I know is that at one time, you said you loved me," I say, forcing myself not to let him see the hurt that he did to me. I'm trying to be strong for me. "And then you didn't."

"I have never not loved you," he says. "It was just ..." Putting his head back, he looks up at the sky and releases a deep breath. "It was a shock. I was in shock when I got that letter. It rocked my foundation. Sitting in my truck, I read the words over and over again, thinking that someone out there was lying. But then the truth hit me in the face, and my whole life or whatever life I thought I had was a lie."

"Nothing was a lie," I say, and he looks at me, shocked that my tone is so angry now. "They didn't lie about the love they gave you. No, they kept a secret, and you don't even know why. You never even stayed to ask why. You just took off."

"You don't know what it feels like to have your whole fucking life flash before your eyes and suddenly feel like you don't know who you are," he says, throwing his hands up. "You don't know what it's like to wonder who you really were. I wonder if my birth father raised me instead of Jacob, would I be this same person? Who the fuck would I be?" His voice goes down. "I didn't know who I was at that moment." He runs his hands through his hair. "So, you don't know, Em."

"You're right; I don't know," I say. "I will never know. But

..." I look down, and the tears come and sting now. "I know a couple of things. Your mother and your father love you with everything. They gave you everything."

"It's not that easy," he tries to tell me. "You just don't know. I had to find out who I was."

"I hope that you found out who that man was because the Ethan I knew was pretty fucking spectacular. That Ethan would *never* bring pain to the people he loved. That Ethan wouldn't just throw me aside as though I was a piece of garbage or yesterday's paper by the side of the road. The Ethan I knew would have held my hand and let me help him through it. The Ethan I know would have been man enough to face this head-on."

"I never ever meant to hurt you." He wipes his own tears. "I never meant to hurt anyone. You will never know what it's like to doubt your existence. How could I marry you without knowing who I was? I couldn't do that to you. I couldn't do it to myself. How could I be a man to you and a father to our children if I doubted my whole life?" He looks at me. "I was never going to come back. In my head, Ethan McIntyre died that night." He trails off the last words.

"He isn't the only one who died that night." I want to be so strong but can't as I relive it. "You walked away that night, and I chased the car." He looks at me shocked. "I ran as fast as my legs would let me. I ignored the burning that I felt in them. I saw you throw the phone out of the window and speed up even faster. I ran until my lungs burned, and then I fell in the middle of the road, and all I could do was watch the two red lights disappear into the darkness while I cried out your name. While I begged you to come back. I didn't move from the middle of the street for a long time. I waited for you to come back. I waited for you, and you never came."

His tears run down his face freely now, but this is what he wanted. This is everything that he asked me for, so I'm going to say my piece, and then it'll be over. "You know what I know?" My shoulders go tight. "I know what it feels like to have half your soul ripped from your body, no, sorry ..." I shake my head. "Your whole soul ripped from your body. Do you know what it's like to have to be picked up off the ground when your legs can't manage to stand because of the pain in your heart? Do you know what it's like to beg and plead for someone to come back? Do you know what it's like to look around and feel like you're a shell of a woman? Do you know what it's like to live in a town when people look at you with pity because you just can't fucking let go of the man who doesn't even want you?" I sob out, and he takes a step forward, but I take a fast step back, holding up my hand. "Do you know what it's like to beg his mother to buy his house, with the hopes that he will come back? Do you know what it feels like to be told time and time again that you have to move on? Being told every single day that you have to start living again, but you can't because the only way you can live is with the one person who doesn't want you. So, you weren't the only one who died that night, Ethan."

"Emily," he says my name in a whisper.

"No." I shake my head. "Those are the last tears I will cry for you, Ethan," I say. "The last. Do me a favor and let me be. If you ever cared about me at all, just let me be."

He walks to me now, and I don't move, I can't. "I'll let you be," he says the words. "But for the record, I loved you every single day that I was gone. I loved you every single second. In my darkness, you were my light," he says words that cut me to the core. "In my pain, you were my strength, and when I looked into the face of evil and fought for my life, you were the reason I wanted to live." My mouth opens, but just like I gave him my truth, he gives me his. He pulls his wallet from his back pocket and takes out a ratted old picture. "The color has faded with all the times it's been taken out and touched, but this picture." He turns it, and I see it's a picture that we took together. He's kissing my neck, and I'm laughing. "This picture saved me in more ways than one." His hand comes out now to touch my face, his thumb wiping away a tear that is running down my face. "I loved you then, I'll love you forever, but I'll let you be." He bends down, and my whole body shakes. "Be happy, Emily," he says, kissing my cheek and walking away from me.

I watch him walk until I can't see him anymore, then turn and walk into the house. My body feels like it's been beaten down. I walk into my bedroom and walk over to the drawer, lifting up the shirts until I find the same picture that he showed me outside. But mine is still in the frame. I look at the picture, bringing it to bed with me, and here in the darkness, I hold it to my chest and cry myself to sleep.

Twelve

ETHAN

As I walk away from her, my heart shatters in my chest, and my mind goes around and around. I don't know how I make it back to the house. Numb. That is the only word I know to describe what this feeling is. I don't bother turning on the lights in the house before I make my way over to where I know the whiskey is kept. Without bothering with a glass, I take a pull straight from the bottle until the burning hurts so much I gasp out, wiping my mouth with the back of my hand. "What the fuck was I thinking coming back here?" Sitting down on the couch, I put my head back and close my eyes, but all I can see is Emily. The pain in her eyes, the hurt in her words, the destruction I left behind. I take another pull of the whiskey. When I left, I thought of none of that. I just thought about myself.

Walking away from them was so hard, but I had to do it for me. I was lost, so lost, and I didn't know where to turn. I walked into church one night. I was dripping wet from the rain that was coming down outside. It was a mirror to how I was doing inside me. I was drowning, my head was under the water, and there were no lifelines thrown in my direction.

Sitting in the last pew in church, I looked up, not even sure what I was doing there. I was hoping I would get the answers I needed. I sat there for much longer than I needed to, and one of the parishioners came over to me.

"Son, you look lost," he said as he sat down next to me. I didn't say anything to him. "I know that look," he said to me, looking ahead. "I've had the same look."

"How did you get found?" I asked, not expecting his answer.

"Military," he said proudly. "Band of brotherhood. Strangers one minute, family the next. I would die for each and every one of them." He said the words, and when I walked into the recruitment office the next day, I felt like a piece of my puzzle was back in its place.

The sound of thunder makes me open my eyes just in time to see the lightning come through the window. I take another pull of the whiskey as Emily's words replay in my head. The whiskey numbs the pain, and when I finish the bottle, it slips from my fingers at the same time as my eyes close and the thunder crashes again.

"Stay down!" Trevor yells from behind me, and the sound of bombs explode all around us. We are going in for a rescue mission. We were given orders eight hours ago, and they just dropped us. But they were ready for us.

"Let's go," Jason says from beside me as we get on our stomach and keep our head down. My heart pounds in my chest. We trained for this, and we are the best of the best for this. We both looke up at the same time, scanning the area to see where the other members are. We've been together for the last three years. My brothers, the ones I walk beside, the ones who carry me on their shoulders.

"On three," he says. I get ready, and on three, we all spring into action. My gun is ready to fire, and I look over, seeing all of us dressed the same as we make our way to the building. It happens so fast that none of us see it. The first bomb strikes near

us, and my ear buzzes right away as we are thrown off our feet. My head hits hard, and all I can hear is more bombs around us.

"Fuck, I'm hit." I hear from beside me, but I can't move. I try to keep my eyes open, but they shut as the sound of bullets whizz around me. I must be hit, I think to myself. This is it. I feel myself being carried and think it is the end, and the only thing that flashes through my head is Emily. I hear voices around me, and then I'm thrown on the ground, and I hear four more thuds.

They start talking in Arabic. "Four are dead," one of them says.

I keep my eyes closed as I hear footsteps walk away. I make the mistake of opening my eyes, and one of them kicks me in my ribs. I'm about to say something when the same foot that kicked my ribs aims for my face.

I wake up yelling with my body trembling. My T-shirt is soaked through with sweat, and it takes me a second to look around and get my bearings. I try to get up, but my knees are still weak, so I fall right back down. I force myself to walk to the bedroom where I take an ice-cold shower. My hands rub the scars that the mission left me with. Scars that made me see so many things and want to come back home. I don't bother going back to bed; instead, I head to the gym and push my body, and when the sun comes up, the barn door opens and Casey comes in.

"Got your text," he says to me, and I can see he's been up a while. "What the fuck were you doing up at three thirty in the morning?"

"Thinking," I say, dropping the dumbbells I'm holding. I don't tell him that the nightmare kept me up all night or that I still have flashbacks. I will, just not yet.

"You know that it is never a good thing," he says, walking in and looking around at all the equipment. "This gym was a good idea. Olivia's idea." He smiles. "She has the best ideas sometimes."

"I'll thank her the next time I see her," I say, and then I grab the water bottle. "I want to know everything." He just eyes me. "I want to know everything you told them."

"Does it matter?" He puts his hands on his hips.

"Yes," I say, looking out at the sun now high in the sky. "If I'm going to mend bridges, I need to know what you told them."

"If you are going to mend bridges, the first thing you have to do is decide if you're staying or going." He glares at me. "It's fine to visit and all that, but—"

"I'm staying," I say. I don't tell him that I made the decision the minute I stepped foot back into town.

"For good?" he asks, and I nod, making it official. "What changed your mind? Five months ago, you wouldn't even entertain the idea of coming home."

"What matters is that I'm here to claim my life back," I say, not ready to go into why. "I need to find a house," I say, and he just shakes his head. "You can't just give me your house."

"But you'll be doing me a favor." He tries to persuade me.

"I'll take the help for now, but I want to earn my keep," I say, and he just smiles. "Why does that smile make me scared?"

"How are your rodeo skills?" he asks, and I just glare at him, putting my hands on my hips. "Perfect, you have a class tomorrow at eight a.m. I'll send you the details." He claps his hands and starts to walk out of the barn.

"Casey!" I shout his name. "You didn't answer my question."

"And I'm not going to." His hand is on the door. "You want to know what I told them, find out yourself." He walks out but then stops. "Hey, Ethan?" He calls my name, walking backward. "Welcome home." He smirks and walks back to his truck. I watch him leave, and when I go inside, I make the second most important phone call of the day.

∾

I'm parked in front of the school, and I hear the bell ring. I get out of the truck and lean against it while I wait for Chelsea. I look around as the kids slowly start piling out. I spot her right away as she walks out, surrounded by three girls I recognize. One of them notices me and points me out, making her look over at me. I raise my hand to say hello, but she just glares at me. Pushing off the truck, I make my way over to her.

"Hey," I say to her and then smile at her friends. They are checking me out, making me feel like a piece of meat.

"What are you doing here?" she asks.

"I thought I could give you a lift home," I say. "Maybe get some ice cream."

"Mom is picking me up," she says. I just smile at her, and she knows that it is a setup.

"She had something come up," I say.

She looks at her friends. "I have to go. I'll text you guys later."

"See you later." I hold up my hand.

"See you later, Ethan," one of them says, and I swear she winks at me. When I turn to walk to the truck, I see Emily walk out of the school, talking with a student. She is dressed in pants and a white button-down shirt today, and her smile fills her face. My heart stops in my chest when I think of everything she told me last night. All I can picture in my head is her kneeling in the middle of the street and having to be carried.

"I can't believe Mom tricked me like that," Chelsea says from beside me, huffing out and making me turn and walk away from Emily. "This is low, even for her."

"Well, we need to talk, and this seemed like a good time," I say, getting in the truck while she huffs out.

"I have nothing to say to you," she says, turning on the radio louder than it should be.

I turn down the volume when we pull out of the parking lot. "Good. Then I'll do all the talking."

"Whatever." She turns and looks out the window. I don't say anything as I turn down Main Street. I put the truck in park and get out, then wait for her on the sidewalk. When we walk over to the ice cream shop, she ignores me as if I'm not even here. She orders her cone, and I order mine, and when we walk to the table, she sits down and looks at me.

I take a big deep breath. "First thing I want to say is that I'm sorry." She just looks at me. "I'm sorry that I left like that."

"Yeah, whatever," she says with all the attitude in the world.

"You have to forgive me," I say, and she looks at me as if I have two heads.

"And why is that?" She takes a lick of her ice cream.

"Because I'm your big brother and because I told you so." I smile when I say those words because I used to tell her that all the time.

"Well, my big brother fucked up," she says softly. It takes everything in me not to go over to her, but I know I have to earn that trust again.

"I did," I agree with her. "I fucked up big time, and I know I have to make it up to you." She just listens to me. "Leaving wasn't the best decision I ever made, but it's a decision that I had to make for me even though that sounds selfish."

"Oh, it's selfish." She agrees with that part.

"I need you to tell me why you are so mad at me," I ask. It's better to come straight out with it instead of beating around the bush. "I can't make it better if I don't know how you feel." I smirk at her. "I get you hate me and want to kick me in the balls, but you need to tell me why."

"You left us." She starts off, her voice low. "Forget the pain you caused Mom, which was a dick move, by the way." She glares at me. "But you just took off on us." Her voice goes soft when she says the next words. "On me."

I swallow the lump that has started to form. "I never meant to hurt you."

"Yeah." She wipes away a tear. "But you did. You were supposed to always be there for me. You were supposed to fight off the boys when they called me. You were supposed to scare away my dates when they came to pick me up. You were supposed to be there." She looks down. "But you weren't."

Looking at her, I go one step at a time. "One, you're dating?" I ask, shocked.

"Seriously, Ethan. From all that I just told you, that's the only thing you picked up on?" she huffs out, and I see a little smile.

"I don't think I'm ready for that." Smiling, I get up and go over to her side of the table. I put my arm around her and bring her to me. "I'm sorry, squirt," I say, and she turns her head and buries her face in my shoulder. She is trying so hard not to cry, but it's getting the better of her. "I'm back now, and I'm going to make it up to you." She cries out now. "No more dating. No more talking to boys. There will be none of that bull. In fact, I think I saw something about nun school." She laughs between her tears.

"I am not going to nun school," she tells me and wipes her tears. "How long are you staying?"

"For good," I say, and she looks at me almost in surprise and shock, her mouth hanging open.

"Does Mom know?" she asks, and I shake my head. "Are you going to tell her?"

"Eventually," I answer her.

"You hurt her really badly when you left," she says. "And she is going to deny it if you ask. But ..." She looks down. "It took her a month to get out of bed. I thought Dad was going to go bald from pulling at his hair. He was helpless. There was nothing he could do. Nothing none of us could do." The words hurt, and she doesn't say anything else. No more words need to be said. I know that I have bridges to mend, and I have to earn everyone's trust back. When I get up from the table, I hold out my hand, and she takes it.

We walk back to the truck, both of us looking down at the road. "So are you really dating boys?" I glance over at her and smile.

"I mean, not a lot of boys." She smiles shyly. "But I am going to senior prom with someone."

"How are you a senior?" I ask, and she just shrugs. "I don't like this one little bit." I put my hands on my hips.

"Well, then you shouldn't have left." She winks at me with a smile, getting in the truck, and for the first time since I stepped foot in town, I have just a sliver of hope.

When I pull up to the house, I see that there are no cars there. "Do you want to come in?" she asks as she reaches for the handle.

"No," I tell her, not sure yet if I can do the whole family dinner. I know I told her that I'm back for good, but I think it's good to go slow. I haven't had the talk with Beau yet, and until then, I'm going to stay clear. "I'm going to head home. Get on the treadmill, work off the ice cream."

She gets out of the car laughing. "Say hi to Mom for me, will you?"

"Will do," she says. I watch her walk into the house, only leaving when she closes the door behind her. When I get to the house, I'm shocked to see my mother sitting on one of the chairs outside. She smiles at me when I pull up. My heart speeds up when I get out of the truck and walk to the front door.

"Mom," I say, and she smiles, getting up and walking over to me. "I didn't know you were coming by." I hug her once I get to the top of the steps. She hugs me a bit tighter than normal.

"I drove by and decided I'd stop and see how you were settling in." She smiles, and I see the tears in her eyes.

"Why the tears?" I ask, and she looks down and then up at me again. This time, her eyes are not able to block the tears.

"I was afraid you'd left," she whispers, wiping away a tear that has escaped.

"I'm not going anywhere," I tell her. "Let's sit down." I point at the chairs. "Or do you want to go in?" She just sits on one of the Adirondack chairs. When I sit down next to her, she reaches out her hand, and I take it in mine.

"Your hand grew," she says, looking at my hand that swallows hers. "So tell me," she says, "what have you been up to?"

I laugh. "When?"

"The past five years," she says, sniffling, and I know she is trying not to cry. "Like what did you do? Who did you hang out with? Did you have any hobbies? Were you with someone?"

I shake my head and look down. "Well, I've been a couple of places, but they are sort of top secret, so all I can say is I traveled."

"I used to pray," she says softly. "When I found out that you joined the military, I used to pray that you would be safe." I nod now. "What about friends? Did you make any?"

"Mom," I say, "I'm twenty-six. We really don't do play dates."

She laughs. "I know, but did you have any friends that, I don't know, celebrated your birthday with you? Who you spent Christmas with?"

"Don't cry," I say, and she just looks at me, and I see her lower lip tremble. "I used to get shit-faced every year on my birthday." She puts a hand to her mouth. "I always dreaded it for so many reasons. One, I was away from you guys, and I just didn't know how to come back."

"It was hard for me, too," she says. "For all of us. Your father," she says, mentioning Jacob, "and I used to sit outside and relive the day you were born." I look down, my heart hurting for both of them. "I was so young," she says. "Young and so scared. I was scared that someone would find out who your birth father was. I was worried that Jacob would tell me he couldn't do it. I was scared that I would fuck all of it up."

"You did what you thought was the best thing at that time," I tell her, and she shakes her head.

"No," she says, "I did the only thing that was right. Yes, I messed up everyone's life. Yes, I was selfish. Yes, I should I have told you. No," she says, "I grew up without a father. My mother would tell me every single chance she got that I was unwanted, and I refused for you to grow up like that. Knowing that your sperm donor didn't want you." She shakes her head. "Fuck no, he didn't deserve you."

"It's okay, Mom," I say. "It took me a while to see that you did it for me." I smile at her. "So thank you."

"Now," she says, "tell me about where you lived."

"I had a little house," I tell her, "or more like a shack. It barely has water, but when I got leave for a month, I used to go up there and fix it up."

"That sounds like fun," she says. "What are you going to do?" she asks, and I just look at her.

"Being back home."

"I'm back, Mom." I lean forward and rest my elbows on my knees, looking out. "For good."

"I'm so happy you're back," she says, "but ..."

"I know," I start, "things are not the same."

"People moved on." I know that by people she means Emily.

"We'll see," I say.

"Well, if it's meant to be," she shrugs her shoulders, "it'll be."

"I can die trying." I roll my lips.

"Can no one die?" She crosses one leg over the other. "Will you stay even if you don't have her?"

"It'll be hard." I feel a tightness in my chest. "I don't know if I'd be able to, but this is my home."

"Sure is," she says, looking out. "This is your home."

"This is my home," I repeat. Neither of us says anything more and just sit with each other. It took me five years to get back here, and every single day is going to be one step in getting my life back.

Thirteen

EMILY

"**Y**ou seem out of it," Drew says two minutes into our daily phone conversation. He's been gone for three days already, and I have to admit it's a good thing he isn't here. I am out of it in every sense of the word.

"Yeah, I had a rough couple of days," I say the truth or at least a part of the truth. "I always get like this toward the end of the school year. You know this."

"I guess I never noticed," he says, breathing out. "I miss you." I want to roll my eyes. Maybe it's because I feel stabby since I've slept maybe five hours in three days, but I'm just annoyed. "Did you think about coming to visit me this weekend?"

"I told you that I couldn't," I remind him. "I have so much to prepare for, not to mention the carnival at the end of the month, and I promised the kids I would help with prom."

"Goddammit, Emily," he snaps. "When are you going to put you and me before your job?"

"So, this is me ending this conversation," I say. "I'm tired, I'm stressed, and frankly, I don't have time for your tantrum."

"I know what this is," Drew says. "I knew the minute he stepped foot into town that you would change."

I gasp out in shock. "I have not changed," I answer. I haven't changed at all. Is my heart intact? No. Am I going on with it? Yes. "And for your information, if you think back to last year, you will recall we had the same argument."

"It's just ..." he starts to say, his voice softening, and I'm over it.

"It's nothing. You're tired, and I'm tired, so I'm going to let you go. I'm going to take a nice bath, and I'll call you tomorrow," I say, closing my eyes.

"Fine," he breathes out heavily. "I'm going to go to the bar to get a drink, and then I'll hit the hay."

"Night, Drew," I say, and I hang up before he says he loves me. Putting the phone on the counter, I get up and walk toward my bedroom. I love my bedroom, and when it came time to decorate it, I did what I wanted. So my king-size bed sits in the middle of the room with a soft pink fabric headboard. The white duvet is so puffy and thick it looks like a cloud. I love pillows, so there are eight pillows on the bed, not counting my light pink throw pillows.

Walking to the closet, I kick off my shoes before walking into the bathroom and going to my tub. I start the water, throwing in a bath bomb. After I undress, I slip into the water and tie up my hair, and a tear falls without me knowing or feeling it. Tears have come every single day since he walked away from me. Or I guess I walked away from him this time. I put my head back and close my eyes, but it does nothing to help with the tears. Instead, it takes me back to memories of him, and I don't want them.

After a mere ten minutes, I get out of the bath and slip on my robe. I walk out and sit on my bed, reaching over and grabbing the remote. I stop and open the white side table drawer, seeing our picture right on the top. I pick it up and look at it again. I want to throw it out, but I know that the minute I do that, I'll regret it.

"Maybe that is what I need," I tell myself, getting out of the bed. "I need to purge him from the house."

I'm about to walk into the closet when the doorbell rings. I look at the clock and see it's only seven fifteen. "Jesus, what is wrong with me?" Walking to the door, I open it and see it's Jenna.

"Are you in your pjs?" she asks, walking in and looking at me with disdain. "It's seven."

"Yeah, well, I'm tired," I say, closing the door. "I didn't know you would be stopping by."

"I know. It's called being spontaneous." She laughs, as we walk down the hallway. "Oh my god, were you making tea?"

"No," I lie to her. "I made tea before the bath."

"You already had a bath? What is wrong with you?" Jenna throws her hands in the air. "Why are the drapes closed? You hate them closed."

I roll my eyes. "I don't hate them closed. It's nighttime."

"The sun is still out." She points at the window as she opens the drapes. "The sun hasn't even set yet."

"I'm tired!" I yell, throwing up my hands. "I haven't slept well, and I'm tired."

"Go get dressed and let's go get some ice cream," she tells me. "You need to get out and not dwell in this fucking house." She glares at me now. "I know what you're doing."

I shake my head. "He told me he loves me." The tears come now as I tell her some of what he told me. I keep most of it to myself, though, because it's mine and only mine.

"When did he tell you this?" she asks quietly.

"Yesterday," I say. "He came to talk to me after the barbecue."

"Asshole," she mumbles. "Go get dressed. We definitely need ice cream."

"I don't want to go," I say. "I have ice cream here."

"I want you to go and get dressed, or I'll dress you myself."

"I don't know why we are even friends," I huff out, stomping to my bedroom with her behind me. I don't have time to grab the picture and put it away before she sees it.

"You kept this?" She sits on the bed and holds the picture in her hands. We shared a dorm room when we were in college, and I kept this picture beside my bed.

"I kept it all," I say as I walk to my closet and take down the box that says riding gear all over it. When I walk back into the bedroom, she looks at me with her mouth open. "Before you came in, I decided I was going to get rid of it." I put it on the bed and open it up, and the minute I do, I know it's going to be the end of me. There on top of the box is his shirt that I wore every single night to bed for a year. I refused to wash it because I was scared that his smell would go away. I bring it to my nose and tears fall on it before I smell it.

"You haven't washed this shirt in five years!" she shrieks from the bed. "That's fucking gross."

"You can still smell him." I smile and hold the shirt out for her, but she backs away from it.

"I'll take your word for it." She grimaces, and I laugh, putting it aside.

Taking out the pictures that are on the top, I flip through them. I'm in his arms in all of them, and he looks at me with a huge smile or I look back at him. "This one is my favorite," she says, taking the picture she took one morning when we were on the beach.

We had stayed at the beach for the weekend, and I begged them to watch the sunrise with me. It wasn't even a warm day, and the wind was blowing fierce. I had to put on one of Ethan's sweaters just to keep warm. Ethan sat on the sand and opened his legs for me to sit between them. I sat down with my back to his chest. He put his arms around me, and I leaned back into him. The sun slowly peeked out of the darkness, and the sound of the waves crashing into the sand filled the early morning quietness.

"Look how pretty that is." I point at the sun coming up at the same time that Jenna took the picture. The sunrise was a light purple, and with my hair blowing and his face by mine, it was magical.

"It was a good day," she says as I sit down.

They were all good days, I think to myself, until the one really bad one, and then, all the good left. Putting the pictures down, I walk over to my closet and slip on a pair of skinny jeans and a white V-neck T-shirt, then slide on my white Vans. "Where are you going?"

"I'm going to return that," I say, pointing at the box and putting everything inside it. "I don't want it. Maybe this is the thing I need to be set free." I throw my hands up.

"You're going to go and bring him this box from five years ago?" She points at the box, trying not to laugh. "To be set free."

"Yes." I roll my eyes, picking up the box and walking out of the room.

"You forgot this one," she says, holding up the frame on my bed. I look at the box and then look at her and then look at the box again.

"It won't fit." I make the excuse and walk out of the house to her laughter. I put the box into the trunk and make my way over to the house where he is staying. The sun is slowly setting when I pull up to the house. I get the box out of the back and walk up the steps to the front door. I press the doorbell and wait.

My heart is beating so fast that I'm surprised my shirt isn't moving. The sound of it echoes in my ears, and my mouth is suddenly so dry that I feel like I'm swallowing sand every time I try to swallow. I wait for a minute, and nothing happens, and the adrenaline suddenly starts to go away, and I have a slight moment of panic.

"What the fuck am I doing here?" I say to myself and then look at the box in my hands. "Oh, good god, this is a bad idea."

I turn to walk away, hoping that maybe he's not even home. Looking up, I wonder if there are cameras, and then I close my eyes tight. Obviously, there are cameras. This is Casey's house.

"Fuck," I hiss to myself, and when I take one step down from the step, I hear the lock open. I look down and wonder if the earth can open and swallow me right about now. I also make a mental note to kill Jenna for not stopping me.

"Em." He says my name, and I turn around, coming face-to-face with him. He's wearing shorts that go low on his hips and nothing else. His hair is wet, and he still has drops of water on his chest.

"I was in the shower," he says, but all I can do is look at him, my eyes roaming his chest as if I've never seen him naked before. My eyes fall on the scars that he has on the side of his ribs. "Did you need something?" he says.

"Um …" I look up at him and see his smirk. Fine, he knows that I love his body. It's not like I kept it a secret when we were dating, but I hate him now so there is that. "I came to return your things."

"My things?" he says, and I hand him the box. "These are yours. I couldn't give you them before, so I thought I would return them now." He just looks at me. "Take the box," I say, raising my voice.

He grabs the box. "Do you want to come in?"

"No. I just came to give you back your things," I say, turning and walking away.

"I'll ask my mom for your stuff," he says, and I stop on the step.

"No need to. She returned it to me five years ago," I say and see the shock on his face. I make my way back to the truck without stumbling and pull away from the house. He watches the whole time, and when I'm finally out of sight, I let the tears fall.

Fourteen

ETHAN

I watch her drive away, and only when I don't see her anymore do I walk back inside the house, going straight for the couch. I sit with the box on my lap, just staring at it.

When I was in the shower and heard the doorbell, I thought I was hearing things until she rang the bell again. I rushed out, not expecting her when I opened the door.

She was one step away from bolting, and her face looked so beautiful that it literally took my breath away. I couldn't understand why she was here, and I wanted nothing more than for her to come in so we could talk. I was hoping she'd come over so we could talk. I never expected her to be returning all my stuff.

My hands shake as I open the lid to the box and find my T-shirt right on top. Picking it up, I run my hands over it. She used to wear this all the time to bed. She would make me wear it when I was over and then cuddle up to it when I would leave. Placing it beside me, I see the pictures next, and everything hits me right away. I take them out and look through them. The picture of us on the beach with the purple sunrise was the day I knew in my heart that she was the one. I mean, I knew before then that she was the one, but at that moment, watching her as her eyes lit up when the sun rose just cemented that there was no one else I wanted to be with. There was no one else for me, and I knew it then. I know it even more now.

There is one of my class books and some random papers that I left over there, but in the bottom corner is the brown velvet box. My heart beats so fast in my chest I have to move the box off my lap. My mouth is suddenly dry and my palms sweaty. Opening the box, I see the engagement ring sitting in the middle of it. My hand moves to take the ring out of the box, and I hold the ring between my thumb and forefinger. Looking down at the ring, I remember the day I gave it to her.

"Sunrise," I whispered when my alarm went off at four thirty that morning. I didn't plan to drive up and see her, but with the ring in my pocket, I didn't want to wait another minute. I kissed her neck. "Sunrise." She turned over this time and cuddled into me like she always did when she didn't want to get up. "I have a surprise for you," I said, and she groaned. Moving her hand down, she grabbed my cock. "Not that surprise." I laughed at her and pushed her hand away. It took one touch from her, and I lost all my senses.

I scrambled to get out of bed as I hopped over her. I put my T-shirt on and then slipped on my jeans. "Why are you getting dressed?" She opened one eye this time. "You don't have to leave for another two hours."

"I want to watch the sunrise with you," I told her, and her eyes lit up as she smiled. "So get dressed." She got up and put on sweatpants and my shirt. She slipped on her flip-flops and grabbed my hand. We walked to our special part of the grass, and she sat in front of me as usual. I pushed her hair aside and kissed her neck right beneath her ear. "I love doing this with you."

"It's my favorite time of the day," she said as she laid her

head back on my shoulder far enough for me to kiss her. "Every day with you is my favorite." She looked ahead as I waited for the sun to peek out from the horizon.

When I saw the little yellow start to come out, I moved into place. I got in front of her on one knee, but she didn't know what was going on until I took the box out of my pocket. "Sunrise." Tears poured down her face, and she put her hands in front of her mouth. "I want to do this with you every single day for the rest of my life. I want to sit with you on our porch and watch every sunrise with you. I want all my days to start with you by my side." I slid the ring on her finger. "Will you be my wife?" All she could do was nod her head.

I put the ring back in the box and make my way to the bedroom. I can't explain to anyone how this moment feels. I feel almost empty. When I left her behind, I closed myself off. I locked it down and never looked back, but now seeing her, being near her it's so much more than I ever thought it would be. I collapse in the bed, and tonight, the nightmares are almost unbearable, so when I wake up gasping for air at four a.m., I give up and head over to the gym. I work out while the sun rises, and at seven fifty-five, I show up at the barn.

"Look who it is," Quinn says, walking out of the barn. "Dad said you would be coming in."

"Did he?" I look at him and see that he looks exactly like Casey when he was younger. "Where is he?"

"He had a meeting with Mom somewhere," he says, "but he said you would know what to do." I nod my head and look at the training facility where I spent most of my time. I would train before school, and I would train after school on the weekends and all summer. I lived, breathed, and dreamed rodeo. Walking into the training arena, I look up at the banners that are hanging. Some of them because of me and I smile. "Does it look the same?"

I go in a circle and look up and around, the whiteboard in

the middle of the room. "It does." I look at the side where the bulls are in their own separate pens. "How many train in the morning?" I ask.

"Today, it's just the three of us," Quinn says, going over to the stands and then grabbing his gloves. "Keith and Reed are going to be here in twenty minutes."

He walks over to the chute area as one guy loads a bull in its place. I walk over and introduce myself to him, and five minutes later, I'm watching Quinn come out of it. He is bounced off after two seconds. I walk over to him and give him a couple of pointers, and when he tries it again, he stays on longer. When Keith and Reed come into the door, they stop and just look at me.

"Get ready, Reed, you're up next," I say, and he just nods, going over to the stands and putting down his bag. He comes back with his gloves on and all he does is listen to my instructions. When it's Keith's turn, I see Reed and Quinn sitting there taking in the notes I'm giving him. After two hours of training, the boys grab their bags and head out. Reed stays behind for a second and comes up to me. "What's up?"

"Chelsea said she spoke with you," he starts. "She says that you're sorry about leaving."

"I am," I say, walking over and grabbing a water bottle and downing it all. "I can't regret the path I took because it led me to the military, but I am sorry that I didn't keep in touch."

"I heard you were badass," he says, taking his own drink of water. "Will you tell me about it sometime?"

"Anytime you want," I say. He nods and then runs to the truck, but I call his name. "Reed."

He turns around. "Did Chelsea tell you to be nicer to me?" I ask, wondering why his attitude changed overnight.

"She might have," he says. "Mom also told me I had no choice."

"Well, I'm happy that we can get to know each other," I say. "See you later."

"See you." He turns and jogs to Quinn's truck, getting into the back. I'm watching them drive away when Casey comes driving down. After he parks and gets out, I see he's wearing a suit.

"You're a little overdressed for the rodeo there, big guy," I joke, and he smirks.

"My wife likes when I dress up for her." He winks at me.

"That's fucking gross," I say, and he just laughs at me.

"How did practice go?" he asks, and I nod.

"Quinn's good," I say. "He needs more confidence in himself, though. He needs to stop second-guessing himself."

"I told him the same thing." He smiles. "Boys need a coach. I need a coach. I need someone who's riding on bulls and who's good with horses. Basically, I need the best of the best." He crosses his arms over his chest. "I'm the best there is."

"Maybe thirty years ago," I joke. "But don't you have a coach?"

"We did, we do, but he's not interested in training the kids anymore. He wants to just do the stuff around here."

"So he doesn't want the dirty work." I shake my head. "When do you have to know?"

"What else do you have going on?" he asks, turning to get into his truck. "We are having dinner at our house. See you tonight at six."

"Um, I was thinking that I would ease into family functions," I say.

"Good. See you at six." He doesn't let me answer before he climbs back in his truck.

I show up for dinner, and it's just Casey and his family. It's not as bad as I thought it would be, and talk is very neutral.

The next day, I get to the arena earlier and make notes for

the boys. The week flies by, but something doesn't sit well with me. Every night, I get home, shower, cook, and sit looking over the pictures over and over again. I look out the window, seeing the stars in the sky, and I make a rash decision. I should think about this before I go over there, but it's been five days, and I haven't seen her or heard her voice.

Walking up the steps, I see that there is a light on inside. I ring the doorbell, but no one comes to the door. I ring it again, and this time, I peek into the windows. I don't see anyone there, but the light on, and her car is parked in the driveway. I don't even know her number to call her, so instead, I walk around to her backyard. As soon as I turn around the corner, I see her lying in the hammock looking up at the stars. I wonder what she's thinking about. I wonder if she thinks of me sometimes. I wonder if she's ever sat looking up at the stars and told me how her day was going like I used to do to her. She must sense me here because she looks over at me and looks shocked that I'm here.

"What are you doing here?" she asks, getting out of the hammock. I see that she's wearing yoga pants and a big T-shirt. Her neck is totally exposed, making me want to kiss her right under her ear. I wonder if she still giggles when you get too close to her ear. "I can't do this with you."

"I want my stuff back," I say, and she looks at me, her eyebrows pinching together.

"I gave you your stuff back." She shakes her head. "Everything that I had of yours was in the box." She walks away from me now toward the door of her house. She puts her hand on the door handle, and I finally speak.

"That isn't what I'm talking about," I say, and she looks over her shoulder. "My mother returned your things five years ago. Those were mine, and I want them back." Her mouth opens. "I want it all back."

Fifteen

EMILY

"I want it all back," he says the words, and I tighten my hand on the handle of the door. This week has been an emotional roller coaster. I've had so many up and down moments that I was counting down the hours until tonight. Until the weekend when I could stay in my house and recharge my batteries. Next week is going to be better. "I want everything that is mine back." I snap at that last sentence and turn around going to him now.

Standing on the top step and looking down at him, I remember how I used to stand and look at him and how he used to take my breath away. But now, I'm seeing him with his white shirt on, his tattoo on his forearm, the hard look in his eyes, and his muscles much bigger than before. His legs are thicker than last time. Now not only does he take my breath away but he also stops my heart, and I hate it. "You are never getting it back," I spit at him. "I don't know what game you're playing, Ethan, but I'm not playing it with you."

"I would never play that game with you, Em," he says the words so soft, and then he trails off at the end when he says my name, shaking his head. "Never. Not before and not now, especially with you."

"Then what the fuck is this?" I throw my hands up. "This is the third time you've shown up at my door. Three. I thought after I told you that you shouldn't be here, you would respect me and just let me be." I take a deep inhale. "Why can't you just leave me alone?" My voice gets higher, and I take one step down, closer to him. "Do you think this is easy for me?" I don't even know if I'm asking him or telling him. "Do you think seeing you doesn't do anything do me? Do you think it's easy for me? I can't keep doing this with you." I'm almost pleading him. "I don't want to do this with you. You left me." I point at my chest. "You left me," I repeat. "So you don't get to be hurt or angry or want things. You don't get that."

"Just because I left doesn't mean I didn't hurt," he says, and I wonder if his hugs would make me feel just as they did before. I wonder if I would feel invincible as long as I was in his arms. I wonder how many other people felt that in his arms, and then I shake my head as the tears start to sting my eyes.

"Being away from you was the hardest thing I ever did." He shakes his head and looks down. "But I had to do it for me. I had to find out what kind of man I was." He puts his hands on his head. "How could I be the right man for you if I didn't even know what man I was inside me?" He puts his hands on his chest, and for the first time, I see the turmoil he must have gone through. "I was lost." His voice is almost broken. "I was empty, Sunrise." I don't tell him not to call me that; I just listen to him. "No matter how much I loved you, I didn't love me."

"Why can't you just let me be?" I blink away the tears, but one escapes, and it slowly rolls down my cheek. "Why can't you just let me be? I was moving on." I put my hand on my stomach to calm the nerves down, ignoring the fact that I used the past tense instead of I am moving on. "I'm engaged, and I'm getting married. I have a right to be happy."

"Do you love him?" When he asks his question, my heart beats so hard and so fast in my chest that I think for sure he is going to hear it. "I just need to know if you love him." He puts one hand on the railing.

"Why are you doing this?" I shout. I don't stop myself. "Why?"

"Tell me you love him." He almost dares me.

"Will that make you leave me alone?" I ask, and he looks down, but when he looks up again, I get lost in his eyes. "Will you walk away and leave me alone if I tell you that?" I don't wait for him to answer.

"I love him," I say in a soft whisper, and I turn to walk into the house. I slam the door this time, locking it behind me. I turn off all the lights and force myself not to open the door again. I force myself not to go to him and ask if he found someone. I try to force myself not to even think about him, but I fail at that one.

I sit in the bathtub until the water turns cold. The only thing I can see in my head is his eyes, his look. The way he spoke of how he felt when he left, and the desperation in his words to be the man who I know he is. When I slip into bed naked, I look over at the red numbers glowing on the clock and see it's almost eleven.

I turn over, checking my phone, and see that Drew didn't call me. He called this morning, and when I told him that I wasn't coming out to see him, he was angry and hung up on me. I was done with his attitude, so I didn't call him back. But I did text him when I got home just to tell him, and he hasn't answered me back. I open my text again and send him another one.

Me: Going to bed. Call me tomorrow.

I look at the phone to see if the white bubble comes up

with the three dots, but it doesn't. Placing it back on the side table, I turn and close my eyes.

My dreams are all of Ethan—his smile, his touch, his laughter, his hugs, and his kisses. And when I finally wake up, tears have soaked my pillow. Turning over, I see it's almost six, so I get up, slip on my robe, and walk to the kitchen. I start my coffee, and when my cup is full, I open the back door just in time to see him walking away from my house. I stop in my tracks. *Did he stay here all night?* He must sense me because he turns around and spots me standing here. "I didn't mean to stay," he says from beside the hammock. "I just wanted to make sure you were okay. I must have dozed off." He looks down and then up. "I'm sorry," he says and walks away from me. As I watch him walk away from me, I press my hand on my chest over my heart. I sit down on the stoop and watch him walk away as the sun comes up.

I try to keep myself busy and my mind off Ethan. After I clean the house, I make a list and head to the grocery store. I'm unloading the car when I see Jenna pull up. "Aren't you lucky?" I say. "Just in time to help me unload the car."

"Oh, goodie." She smiles at me and helps me unload my car. "How much shit did you buy?"

"This is what happens when you go shopping and you're starving," I say, putting five of the bags on the counter. "This right here."

She laughs and helps me put away the stuff. "He came here last night," I say when she sits on the stool at the counter drinking tea. I avoid her eyes as I cut up the fresh strawberries. "Then this morning, I went out to watch the sunrise, and he was still here." She gasps. "I just want to be able to see him and not care."

"That is never going to happen," she tells me, grabbing a strawberry, and I look at her shocked. "What?" She shrugs. "You think that you won't ever be thinking what-if every single time you see him?" I don't answer her. "Every single time you see him, what-if is going to fly into your head. No matter how much you say you love Drew."

"I thought after I laid out my heart to him and told him how much he hurt me that I would be okay with it," I say, tossing a strawberry in my mouth, and she just looks at me. "Okay, fine, I'll have the what-ifs, but it won't change anything."

"Step one is admitting it." She laughs. "I want to go to the bar tonight."

"No," I say right away. "No fucking way. I had the shittiest week of my life."

"Exactly." She points at me. "Let's get dressed up and go dancing. God, we haven't done that in a while."

"We did that last month," I remind her. "Brett had to carry you out over his shoulder." I point at her, and she shrugs.

"We need to go out. You need to get your mind off him, and nothing will do that like tequila and some line dancing." She puts her hands in the air and dances. She takes her phone out of her pocket and calls Brett, who answers after one ring, "Hey, baby," she says softly, and he groans.

"Nothing good comes when you start a conversation that way," he says. "Hurry up, I'm up next."

"We are going to go dancing tonight, so dust off the cowboy boots," she tells him.

"Fuck, Jenna, I thought we were doing Netflix and chill. More chill than Netflix," he says, and she smiles.

"After all that tequila, we can chill all night long," Jenna tells him.

"You guys are gross." I fake vomit and turn to walk out of the room to give them privacy. I sit on my bed and try to call Drew. I don't expect him to answer so when he does, I'm shocked and surprised.

"Hey," I say, smiling when I hear his voice. "I didn't think you would answer."

"Hey," he says, and he sounds like he's running. "Sorry about last night." His voice goes low. "I just went to bed early and turned off my phone," he whispers. "I'm at the hotel gym. Can I call you later?"

"Yeah," I say. "Sure. I just wanted to see what you were doing. Call me later."

He hangs up, and I sit on the bed and look at the phone, not feeling right. Maybe I have guilt from seeing Ethan.

I close my eyes, and then I hear Jenna yelling. "I'm going to borrow your clothes." Her voice comes closer to the bedroom, and I look at her. "If I go home, you are going to come up with some excuse not to go, and I'm not letting you."

I don't argue with her because I know that no matter what I say, she isn't going to listen to me. Instead, we watch a couple of movies and pop a pizza in the oven. She takes a shower and slips into my blue jeans and a black cami. I, on the other hand, slip on my jean shorts that show off my long tan legs and grab the white off-the-shoulder cotton shirt. The sleeves are long and tight until the elbow and then flare out. The bottom of the shirt is loose and looks like lace. I slip on my high heel short cowboy boots, and when I walk out of the bathroom, Jenna's mouth hangs open. "Oh. My god."

"I wear this all the time," I say, but I'm lying. I've never worn this shirt, and the jean shorts have always been in my drawer, but I've never had the courage to wear them.

"Lies," she tells me but doesn't say anything else. She just pulls my hand, and we walk out of the house. I drive my car there, and when we get there, the parking lot is full, which is normal for a Saturday night. This bar is the best thing in five counties, which means people rush here on the weekend. I tuck my phone in my back pocket as we walk to the door. The sound of music is already coming out. "We are going to fuck shit up," she says, pulling open the door. I throw my head back and laugh. As soon as I step foot in the building, my body already senses him. When I look through the crowd of people, I spot him behind the bar. He smiles at the woman in front of him as he hands her a beer. I stop in my tracks and Jenna looks in the direction and says exactly what I'm thinking. "Holy shit."

Sixteen

ETHAN

I can feel eyes on me, and when I look up from the bar, I see her. My body tenses. I can count on one hand the number of times I've been knocked back on my ass, and this one right here is on there. She's so fucking gorgeous, and I stare at her not even thinking of the hundred people who are around us. I stare at her, hoping she can hear my thoughts. *It's you. It's always been only you. It will always be you.* "Tell me, Ethan." The girl in front of me says my name, and I look at her. "How long are you staying for?" I don't even know who this woman is, but from the times people say hello to her, she must be a regular here.

"I have no plans of leaving," I say. Pulling the rag tossed over my shoulder, I wipe the bar in front of her before moving down the bar to grab a couple more orders.

"I didn't think you could do it." I hear the guy from beside me. I met him a couple of hours ago when I came in. His name is Scott, and he's been working here for the past five years. "When your mom said you would come in and help, I was shocked and, not going to lie, annoyed."

I pour two shots of tequila and a draft beer, handing it to

the waitress who takes off. "I have been working here my whole life." I look over at him. "I would beg my mother to let me come here when I was fourteen." Wiping down the bar again, I walk over to the sink to rinse it off. "She would always tell me no, but then Beau would miss her like crazy, and he would sneak me in."

Scott laughs as he points at a guy waiting in line. "He's still lovesick over her." He laughs. "When she works two nights in a row, he comes in and doesn't move from that stool over there." He points at the random stool that he has always kept there. "He also gets up and covers her when she bends over. It's hysterical."

I shake my head and smile at the two girls at the end of the bar waiting to be served. "What can I get you?" I ask them but look away into the crowd to see if I see her. She stands now beside the same group of guys I spent the afternoon training with.

"I'll take two Bud Lights with lime," the blonde says to me.

"And I'll take your number," the brunette next to her says, laughing. "Or you can take mine."

I shake my head and turn around to get the two bottles of beer, twisting off the caps and putting it down. "Twelve fifty," I say. "And thanks for the offer."

She grabs the beer and hands me a napkin. "Just in case you change your mind." She turns around and walks away, and nothing inside me moves. Not one single part of me is alive. I grab the napkin and toss it in the garbage.

"That's brutal," the blonde from before says.

I shrug my shoulders. "It is what it is," I say. "Can I get you anything else?"

"I guess your boots under my bed is out of the question?" She winks at me.

"Unless you knock me out cold and take them off my feet," I say halfway down the bar.

"Well, then." She puts money down on the bar. "Have a good night, Ethan. Glad to have you back."

"Who is that?" I ask Scott, who fills me in on the woman who moved here four years ago. She and Mom are friendly, which is how she knew about me. "She's a cougar." He motions with his head toward the group of cowboys that train at the arena. She slides up to one of them, and they don't stand a chance at it. His eyes go cross-eyed when she whispers in his ear. I put my hands on the bar, and I just shake my head and laugh.

"Hey there," I say to Brett when he walks up to the bar. "Fancy seeing you here."

When I went into the arena this morning, I didn't expect the old boys to be there, but apparently, it's a Saturday thing. He just looked at me and didn't say a word. It was only after a couple of hours that he finally spoke to me. "What you did was fucked up." He didn't even start out with small talk.

"I'm aware," I told him. He and I were always friendly when we saw each other, and we saw each other more than we wanted to. With Jenna and Emily being best friends, it was hard to avoid it.

"It wasn't good." He didn't have to tell me what I knew. "Took her a long time to get out there." He was about to say something when his phone rang, and I knew right away it was Jenna. "Motherfucker," he said when he hung up. "We're going to the bar tonight." He looked down. "You still love her?"

I didn't know if I should answer him. I thought about it for one second before my mouth spoke for me. "With everything that I am."

"Thought so," he said. "Don't fuck this up." He looked around. "I want her to be happy. I want to see the sparkle in her

eye that she used to have with you. I love that woman as if she is my sister, and I want her to have what Jenna and I have."

"She told me she loves him." The words burned in my stomach. *The minute she told me that she loved him and walked away from me, I had no choice but to sit down. I wasn't ready for it then, and I wasn't ready to think about it now.*

"I reckon she thinks she does," he said, shaking his head. "He doesn't deserve her. Fuck, I don't even think you deserve her."

"No question there. I don't," I told him, taking a sip from the water bottle I picked up. He agreed with me, and for the rest of the day, we didn't talk about it.

"What can I get you?" I ask. Looking over his shoulder, I see Jenna throw up her hands and grab Emily's hand as they get on the crowded dance floor. Brett looks behind me at them and shakes his head.

"I'll have twenty beers and four shots of tequila," he says and looks over to make sure Jenna is okay, and no one is next to her.

"I'll bring them over to you," I say. "Go stand guard." He doesn't say anything else before he walks away to the dance floor. My eyes can't stop looking at her as she twirls and her hair follows her. It's the first time I've seen her smile like that. I want her to smile like that all the time. I put the beers on the tray and carry over the ten beers first and then go back for the other ten.

I place the tray in the middle of the tall table that the boys are standing next to. They all smile, and one hands me a beer. "Thanks, but I have more drinks to get." Walking back and getting the shots, I wonder who the fuck those are for. I don't have to wait long because Jenna is grabbing them off the tray before I even put it down.

"Here." She hands one shot to Emily, who avoids my eyes as she downs it. I see her wince a bit, and I laugh because she was never a big drinker. I'm not ready for her to take the second shot, but she's wiping her mouth with the back of her hand, and all I can think about is leaning down and kissing her lips. Turning around, I'm walking away when I hear Jenna call my name. "Ethan?" I turn back. "Can you get us six more?"

"Not a chance in hell," I say, and she folds her hands over her chest. "Ask your man if it's okay with him." I turn and walk away when I see Brett glare at her. I also don't make it back to the bar before Brett is there ordering four more shots.

"This is a bad idea," I say. "Does she drink often?" I hate having to ask him a question I should know the answer to.

"Not really, but I'm here, and the guys will watch out for her," he tells me, and we share a look. "Plus, she has you here."

After I prepare the shots for him, he takes them to her, and Jenna and Emily both laugh at him when he tells them something. Jenna looks over at me and holds up the shot of tequila in one hand while flipping me the bird with the other hand. Scott smiles from beside me, and all I can do is shake my head. The whole night I watch her from afar—every single time she lifts her arms, you see a little bit of her tanned stomach, and I have to stand behind the bar to hide my hard-on. She dances most of the night, and when she isn't dancing, she's laughing with the guys, and I have to wonder if Drew makes her laugh like this. Does she laugh until she can't breathe with him? Does she tease him like she used to tease me? I shake my head when the songs turn slow, and I look over and see it's almost two thirty. The bar is finally clearing out. Only the couples and the guys hoping to get lucky remain. I see Brett pulling Jenna to the dance floor when "You Make It Easy" comes on.

I grab a water bottle as I watch her sway side to side, and when Scott calls my name, I look over at him. "I've got this. You can go hang out with the boys," he says. "Thanks for tonight. I'll tell your mom I approve."

I laugh at him. "Thanks for that." I turn back and see that

she isn't there anymore. I scan the whole bar, looking for her. I walk around and go to the back where the pool tables are and still don't see her. When I walk toward the front and still don't see her, my heart starts to panic. She isn't on the dance floor. I turn to walk toward the office, and when I turn the corner, I crash right into her. She almost bounces off me, and I wrap one hand around her to stop her.

She laughs, but I'm not sure she realizes it's me. "I'm sorry," she says, and then her brain must catch up when she sees it's me. Her hands are on my chest, and her heat goes through me. "I wasn't looking where I was going." She stares up at me, her guard down for once. Her eyes hazy from the tequila, her cheeks pink from dancing. "I'll watch better next time," she says with a smile on her face so big that her eyes crinkle at the corners. Her tongue comes out and licks her lips. "You look good," she says. Her thumb moves on my chest, and she looks down at her hands on me. My arms around her don't loosen. In fact, they get tighter. "You always looked good," she says softly.

"Emily," I say her name in a plea, moving my head down slowly as we stand in the dark hallway. The sound of her phone ringing makes her jump out of my arms.

"Oh my god," she says, putting her hands to her forehead. "I'm sorry," she says, taking the phone out of her back pocket. We both look down to see who is calling, and at that moment, everything changes.

"It's Drew," she says, turning and walking out the back door.

Seventeen

EMILY

I can still feel his hands on me when I open the back door and the cool air hits me. The phone ringing in my hand was like an ice-cold bucket of water being thrown on me. "Hello." I say into the phone.

I look over and see that he followed me outside. Everything around me is spinning while I listen on the phone.

The rustling makes it hard to hear and I look down and see that the call is still going on. I see his name, so I didn't imagine it with all the drinks that I've had. I've been drinking all night to take the edge off seeing Ethan there. "Hello?" I say again, only to hear moaning followed by voices.

"*That's it, Drew,*" a woman says, moaning. "*Right there. Fuck, right there.*" I hear what could only be described as grunts. "*Fuck me harder,*" she says, and the phone slips from my hand, crashing to the ground.

My hands shake, and Ethan calls my name, catching me before I hit the ground. "Em," he says my name. "Em."

I can't answer him. I can't do anything. I just shake in the middle of the grass. My phone rings again. He reaches for it this time, putting it on speaker, and the sounds of rustling are apparent right away.

"*Fuck, your pussy is tight.*" I hear the words, then I hear a car horn coming from the car as they both laugh.

"*That's what you get for fucking me in the car,*" the woman says as Drew laughs. "*Every time we fuck in the car, you say that.*"

"I'm going to be sick," I say, and he hangs up the call. The side door opens, and Jenna comes out followed by Brett. She sees me on the ground, and she just looks at Ethan.

"What the fuck did you do this time?" She walks over to him and pushes him, but he doesn't even move. "You fucking destroyed her last time."

"Baby," Brett says from behind her, holding her around her chest. "You need to relax."

"Drew called." I say the words softly, but I have to stop because my stomach lurches in my throat. I have to put my hand down on the grass as my head spins for so many different reasons. I'm hoisted up in his arms before I can even react. My eyes close as my head spins, and all I can do is hear the voices over and over again. "I'm going to be sick."

"You can follow us, but she is not doing this here," Ethan tells Jenna.

"If you think we are going to leave you alone with her," Jenna says. "You're fucking wrong."

He looks down at me. "You need to breathe," he tells me. "Close your eyes and breathe." I feel myself being carried and then placed down on a seat. He puts a seat belt around me, and my phone rings again.

"Don't answer it." I shake my head. "I don't want to hear it." He nods at me, and then the back door to the truck opens, and Jenna jumps in with Brett.

I close my eyes as he pulls away from the bar, and the phone rings again. "Give it to me," Jenna says, reaching over the front seats to grab the phone. She puts it on speaker, and the sound of moaning fills the car.

"*Bite my nipples just like that,*" the girl says, breathing heavily. "*I love it when you fuck my ass.*"

"Hang it up!" Brett and Ethan both yell, and I look over at Ethan.

"I think I'm going to be sick," I say.

"Do you mean you're going to be sick, sick? Like barfing sick?" he asks, driving faster, looking over at me, "or is this like sickening?"

I look at him, and I'm numb. "That motherfucking," Jenna says from the back, and she now calls him. The sound of ringing fills the car.

"What the fuck are you doing?" Brett shouts from beside her, trying to get the phone away from her, but she pushes his hand away from her.

There is the sound of rustling again, and then he whispers when he answers, "Hello? Baby?"

"Baby, my fucking ass!" Jenna yells at him.

"What, who is this?" he asks, confused. "What the fuck is going on?" The sound of rustling fills the car, and I have to close my eyes. "Wait, Jenna? Where is Emily?" he asks, his voice rising.

"I can tell you where she isn't," she snaps at him. "She isn't in the car with you while you fuck her ass, douchebag."

"What are you talking about?" He pretends to be confused. "I don't know what you're talking about."

"Check your call history, dipshit," she says, and she hangs up on him.

The truck comes to a stop, and when I open my eyes, I see that we are at my house. "Can you walk, or do you want me to carry you?" Ethan asks quietly from beside me, and I just shake my head. Slipping open the truck door, I walk up my front steps, then stop at the front door and turn around on them. Ethan is at the top step right behind me while Jenna is being helped by Brett, who is whispering something to her.

"How did I not know?" I look at Jenna and Brett to see if either of them knew anything, but they have no answers whatsoever. "Like how did I never even suspect it?" Ethan stands there with his arms crossed over his chest. Brett stands next to him now, and Jenna is rolling her eyes.

"You didn't even let him see you naked," she says out loud, and I want to kill her. She sees my face and puts her hand in front of her mouth. Then turns to look at the guys. "No one heard that."

"Okay," Brett says. "It's time for us to go." He picks her up and tosses her over his shoulder, then he looks at Ethan. "You got this?"

Ethan nods at him, but his eyes never leave mine. "You don't have to stay," I say as I turn around and go in my house. "Actually, it might be better if you go." He follows me in and walks to the kitchen, grabbing the kettle and putting water in it before turning the stove on. "What are you doing?"

"Making coffee," he says, opening the cupboards. "If I know Drew, he should be here in three hours, depending on where he is." He finally finds the things he needs to make coffee. "And whatever you guys talk about, it should be done with you being semi sober."

"I am sober," I say. "I mean, I'm not going to lie. I was a little buzzed. But nothing like listening to your fiancé fuck someone's ass to sober you up."

He leans against the counter, and my phone starts to ring again. He walks over to it and picks it up. "It's Drew."

"Don't answer it," I say, and he just places it down on the counter. "I don't think you should be here when he gets here."

"I'm not leaving him alone with you," he says, and all I can do is shake my head.

"This has nothing to do with you," I say. I'm about to say something else when we hear a car door slam.

I look at Ethan. "I thought he was out of town." We both turn and look at the front door that swings open, and Drew comes in. He's wearing his suit and a button-down shirt that looks like it's all buttoned wrong. His hair looks like it's been pulled, and he doesn't look like the perfectly kept man who he usually is. His eyes go from me to Ethan and then back to mine.

"Well, isn't this interesting," he hisses when he sees Ethan in the kitchen. "I get now why you wanted to stay home this weekend."

I put up one of my hands now. "Hold on, are you seriously going to turn this around on me?" I ask. "You." I point at him, then to myself. "Cheated on me. I heard all of it."

"Please." He rolls his eyes, putting his hands on his hips. "You've been cheating on me since he got back into town."

"What?" I ask, shocked and appalled.

"Watch it," Ethan growls out.

"Fuck you," he hisses out to him, then turns to me. "You've never gotten over him." He points at Ethan. "Do you know what it's been like for me to wait for you to finally get over him?" I listen to him as his voice gets louder. "We've been together for two years, and you won't even sleep with me." He throws his hands up in the air.

"Hold on a second," I say, now turning to Ethan. "You have to leave." He looks at me, not sure. "I'll be fine. This isn't your problem." He just nods at me and then walks over to Drew and leans down.

"If you hurt her," he says, his voice low, "they won't ever find you." I've never heard Ethan be anything but nice, but nothing is nice about that sentence.

"Why don't you crawl back under that rock you've been hiding under for the past five fucking years?" he says again to

Ethan, who just looks back at me then walks out of the house. I know he isn't leaving. I can feel it in my soul that he won't leave me with Drew. I wait for the door to close before I start talking.

"I never cheated on you," I tell him as tears come to my eyes. "Not once in all the time we were together was I unfaithful to you."

"You're lying!" he shouts. "How many times did you pretend I was Ethan? How many times did you wish I was him?"

"When I was with you, I was with you, Drew. And only you," I say, and since this is over, I don't hold my tongue. "I was with you. I told you from the beginning that my heart was healing. I told you that it would take time. I never lied to you about that."

"Take time." He shakes his head. "How much more time did you need? It's been five fucking years."

"So, the answer to that would be to cheat on me?" I ask. "Instead of waiting for me, or talking it out with me, or better yet, walking away from me, you think it's okay to fuck someone else?" I shake my head. "You had sex with this person, and from the sounds of it, it was not the first time."

He looks down now, avoiding my eyes. "I shouldn't have done it. I know that, but come on." He runs his hands through his hair. "I was like a puppy waiting for a treat."

"I never intended for you to feel like that. I never wanted you to feel that way," I say softly.

"Do you still love him?" he asks. "After all this, after he hurt you so bad, do you still love him?"

"A part of me will never stop loving him." I'm honest with him. "It's the same answer I gave you when you asked me to marry you. Nothing has changed. I don't think anything will ever change that. A part of me will always love him." I shrug. "I was never dishonest about that."

"I guess I always hoped you would love me like that," he says. "I waited and waited."

"Obviously, the waiting was over," I say. I take the ring off and walk to him. "This is yours." I hand it to him, and he shakes his head.

"What are you going to tell people?" he asks, and I want to laugh. He really doesn't even care that he hurt me. He's more worried about what I'm going to say.

"What do you want to tell people?" I ask, and he looks down and then up.

"We can say we grew apart." I nod at him. "I would have loved you with everything I had."

I look at him. "No, you wouldn't." He looks shocked. "If you would have, you wouldn't have done what you did. You wouldn't have looked at someone else." He nods at me and walks out of the house, and just like that, another chapter in my life is over.

Eighteen

ETHAN

I watch him drive away from the backyard, and I'm about to walk up to the door when the lights inside turn off, leaving it in darkness. I sit down and wait to see if she changes her mind, and all I can do is think about how her face was when she found out he was cheating. It was the definition of defeat, her shoulders slumped, and only when he accused her of still loving me did they go up tight again.

I wait another hour, then I finally make myself leave, slipping into bed at close to four a.m. I didn't think I would be able to fall asleep, but when I did, it was the first night without waking up in a pool of my sweat and the sound of myself screaming.

Walking to the barn to work out, I look up and see that the clouds seem to be coming in faster. I open the barn door, leaving it open to get some air in, and I start to work out. I run to clear my mind, but the only thing going through my mind today is Emily. I wonder if she is okay. Did she sleep last night or did she cry herself to sleep?

I don't even notice that I'm sweating through my shirt, and when I stop running to take a drink of water, I take it off, tossing it on the mat. My chest is rising and falling as I drink my water and try to get my heartbeat back to normal. I set the water down and look up to see her walking toward the barn. She is wearing tight blue jeans with holes in the knee and a white loose sleeveless shirt tucked in the front and white sneakers. She looks down as she walks over to me, and only when she feels me watching does she looks up. She almost stops in her tracks, but I raise my hand to say hello.

"Hey there," I say when she is close enough to hear me.

"Hi," she says, putting her hair behind her ear. "I tried the doorbell, but then I heard the music coming from the barn."

"That's fine," I say, and I see that she's wringing her fingers. "Are you okay?"

"I think so," she tells me. "I just wanted to come thank you for last night. You didn't have to do what you did." She swallows now, and I want to wrap my hand on the side of her neck and pull her to me. She looks down and then up again, and I see that she is looking at my scars. "Are you okay?" She points at the scars on my ribs.

I laugh now. "I mean, I'm as good as new." She looks at me. "This?" I point at the scar that is fading from an angry purple to pink. "This is where they shot me."

She gasps. "Who shot you?"

"Um, it's kind of classified." I smirk at her. "But they were not good people."

"I heard that you joined the military," she says, and I nod my head. "I'm glad you're safe."

"Thank you," I say and bend to pick up my shirt. "Do you want to maybe have coffee?"

"I should go," she says, but her feet don't move.

"Are you sure? I was going to make one for myself anyway. How about you sit outside and just relax?" I say, and she walks back with me to the house. She sits outside on the swing hanging under the back porch. I make coffee as fast as the water can come out. The whole time I'm looking outside to see that she is still there. I grab a couple of muffins that my grandmother brought over yesterday. "Em." I call her name, and she comes in. "I don't know how you take your coffee. You never drank coffee when we were together."

"I don't drink it now, either," she tells me and smiles. "I just didn't know how to tell you."

I laugh at her now. "I can make tea." I open the fridge. "I have some tea already made if you want it cold."

"That sounds good," she tells me as I fill a glass. She takes it from me and turns to walk out to sit back on the swing. I walk behind her and sit next to her, rubbing my hands on my legs to make the nerves go away.

"This is weird, right?" she asks, bringing the tea to her lips. "Us sitting here like this."

"I don't think it's weird per se." I smile at her. "Awkward, maybe, but not weird." She looks ahead. "I want to get to know you again," I say, and she looks over at me. "I want to know what your favorite thing to eat is. I want to know that you still don't drink coffee but drink tea. I want to know—" I'm about to say something else when she cuts me off.

"You want to know what you missed in the five years you've been gone." She finishes the sentence for me. "I don't know if I can do that," she says softly. "Getting over you was the hardest thing I had to do in my whole life." Her hands start to shake, and I want to reach out and hold her hand in mine, bringing it to my lips. "I don't know if I can do it again." She wipes a tear away.

"I'm not going anywhere," I say. "I'm staying."

"For how long?" she asks, and I look over at her.

"I told you I wanted it back, and I meant it. I want you back. I want my life back." She is about to say something, but I hold up my hand. "I know I have to earn it back, and that is my goal. I've never gotten over you." I look at my hands. "I wanted to wait before I told you this story, the whole story, but I'll share a little bit of it. I died five months ago," I say, and the tears fall as soon as I say the words. "I died, and the only thing on my lips was your name."

"Ethan." She whispers my name.

"The next time I opened my eyes, I was in a hospital bed. I didn't even know what happened to me until five months later. It came crashing back to me one night in a nightmare. I was back in that dark dungeon of a room lying on the dirt. Lying there with my eyes barely open and the taste of metal in my mouth, I told God that if I survived this, I would come home. I would face my family. I wanted it back. I wanted to hug my mother and tease her for being so small. I wanted to stand by my father and have him be proud of me. I wanted him to slap me on the shoulder and then give me a hug. I wanted to tease Chelsea and Amelia about boys. I wanted to be the one they came to with problems. I wanted to go riding with my brothers, but most of all." I look at her, making sure she sees my eyes. "I wanted to be the man who stood beside you and made you smile. I wanted my life back."

"Ethan ..." she says, and I don't know if she wants to tell me it will never happen. I don't know what she's going to say because the sound of thunder makes her jump. Neither of us says anything as we look out at the rain that is now pouring down. I don't want to say anything in case she decides that she is going to go, so I just sit here and take in the moment. The downpour doesn't last long before the clouds move out, and the sun shines bright. "Okay."

"What?" I look over at her and see that she has tears running down her face.

"Okay, we can get to know each other," she says. "As friends, if nothing more comes of it."

"Was he telling the truth?" I look at her. "Did you never sleep with him?"

She gets up now. "That's none of your business." She puts the glass down and then tries to walk away, but I grab her hand, and she stops and looks down, seeing her hand in mine.

"I haven't been with anyone either," I say and let go of her hand. "I just wanted you to know." She doesn't say anything. She just walks down the steps and around to the front of the house. I want to follow her and see if our kisses still make my whole body come alive, but instead, I give her the space she needs.

~

When I slip out of the truck at my grandparents' house, I look around to see if she is there, but I don't spot her anywhere. I walk in and spot Chelsea with Amelia right next to her. "Why does this look like trouble?" I say, and they both look down. "What did you do?"

"Nothing," Amelia says, trying to hide her smile.

"Absolutely nothing," Chelsea says, and they turn to walk away. I say hello to my grandparents and then go in search of the person I have next on my list to talk to.

I see her right away, laughing with Olivia. I walk up to them and smile at them. "You girls look like Chelsea and Amelia planning something." It makes them laugh even more. "I was wondering if we could talk," I tell Kallie, who just looks at me. "It's fine if you don't want to."

"Of course." She gets up and puts her arm around my waist. "Anything for my boy." I put my arm around her, and we walk away from the noise of kids running and adults talking. "This is nice," she says, hugging me closer to her.

"It is," I say. "I never got to thank you." My arm brings her close to me.

"Thank me?" she asks.

"From the moment you met me, you loved me unconditionally," I say as we near the fence all the way at the end of the property.

"It was love at first sight," she says, and I look at her, her blond hair blowing in the light wind. "You know that, right?"

"I do," I say. "I'm sorry for leaving." My voice comes out softly. "The way I left especially. You ..." I look down. "You were the one most hurt when I was born. You gave up everything for me, and then when you came back, you just loved me with no more questions asked."

"I loved you because you were an amazing young boy," she says, wiping tears away from her eyes. "I also loved you because you were a part of your father, and I loved him with everything."

"How could you?" I ask. "How could you love me when I hurt you so much?"

"You didn't hurt me," she tells me and then grabs my face. "Your father did what he needed to do for you, and I accepted that. Your father would have walked through the eye of the storm for you." The tears slip off her chin. "He's not the same man he was." She shocks me. "He pretends he is, but a piece of him is missing. He still sets the table with an extra plate. He still buys you presents on your birthday and Christmas."

"What?" I ask, shocked.

"Losing Gabriel was hard for him. He mourned the little boy who he created, but losing you, losing you ..." Her bottom lip quivered. "He lost the boy he loved from when you were first placed in his arms. He lost the boy he taught things to, he lost the boy he raised, he lost the man who he helped you become. You can say that he isn't your father, but we both know that isn't true. Just as you can't tell me I'm not your mother. I may not have birthed you, and I may not have held you the first day, but I was the one who used to read you bedtime stories. I was the one who drove you to your practices and held your hand when you were scared. I was the one who waited with bated breath at your rodeos. I was the one who punished you when you snuck out all those times, and I was the one who looked away most times." She winks at me. "To me, that means more to me than what blood runs through you. I ran away once." She swallows. "So I know how you feel. I thought the whole world was against me. I pretended I was okay every single day for eight years. I even convinced myself I was okay until I stepped back into town, and I knew I wasn't okay. You had to run away, and I get it. If anyone can understand it, it's me."

"I was never going to come back," I say, and she smiles.

"Well, whatever brought you back, there had to be a reason," she tells me. "It's what you do going forward that will speak volumes."

"I'm staying," I say, and she crosses her hands over her chest. "For good."

"You are going to make a lot of people very happy." She hugs me now around my waist and places her head on my chest. "You need to talk to him."

"I know," I say. "I do. It's just ..."

"You'll know when it's time. I love you, Ethan, the boy you were, the man you were, and the man you are now," she tells me. "Now why don't we get back there before they send out a search party for us." As we walk back to the barbecue, I know I can scratch another name off my list.

Nineteen

EMILY

I sit in the middle of the couch, correcting the essays from my students last week. I know I should get up and go to the barbecue, but after walking away from him, I drove back home and cried.

Seeing him with his shirt off jilted me a bit, but after seeing the angry scar on his side, I couldn't keep from asking if he was okay. If I hadn't been sitting in the chair when he told me he died, I would have fallen to the floor. My heart dropped out of my chest, and my stomach ached. He told me his story or a piece of it, and all I wanted to do was crawl into his lap and hug him. But instead, I agreed to get to know him, get to know the man who he is now. When I got home, I was shocked to find a box sitting by my door with all the things I'd kept at Drew's.

When I picked it up, I found a letter placed on the top. I didn't know what I was expecting, but it was nothing that was in the letter.

Here is your stuff. If you can get me mine by tomorrow it would be appreciated. Just leave it on the porch.

He didn't even sign his name. I looked at the stuff in the

box, and I had to laugh. He was returning my coffee mug. I shake my head at the couple of shirts I had there, and the one picture he kept in his house. I took everything out and threw it in the garbage, then I walked around the house with the same box and filled it up or at least that was the plan. In the end, the only thing I had of his was a tie. We were together for over two years, and all he had at my house was a tie. I walked into the bathroom and thought maybe I'd find his aftershave or at least his razor, but no. I had more shit that belonged to Brett in my house than I did of Drew. I dropped the empty box by the door and decided to stay in. Jenna called to check on me and after convincing her I was okay, I changed into my yoga pants, grabbed the stack of papers I needed to grade, and then got lost in the stories of my students.

As I start another paper, I hear a soft knock on the door. I thought for sure it would be Jenna, but when I open it, I stand here looking at him. He has a baby blue button-down shirt with the sleeves rolled up to his elbows, making the blue of his eyes stand out even more with his shirt color. I look at the ink on his arms, and I want to touch it so bad. He wears khaki pants with brown boots. "I thought you might need something to eat," he says, lifting the bag that he has in his hand that I didn't even notice. "It's your favorite."

I motion with my hand. "Come in." After I move to the side, he steps in, his eyes going to the box by the door. "You didn't have to bring me anything."

"I know I didn't have to," he says, not moving from the door. "But I wanted to." He smiles, and I try to ignore the way my heart beats, or that the pain in my chest is just a little less since last week. He places it on the counter next to the picture of Drew and me. It's the only thing I kept that was in the box. It was one of our first dates, where we were dressed up to go to his work function. "You look good here," he says, looking at it and then up again. "I mean, you look good in anything." He puts it down, and then he just stares at me.

"What did you bring me?" I ask, grabbing the brown paper bag and finding containers inside. "Is this chicken fried steak with mashed potatoes?" I look at it and then grab another container to find the gravy. "Oh my god." I turn and pop it into the oven and set the timer. "I haven't eaten all day." I walk over to the fridge. "Would you like a beer?"

"Water is fine," he says, and I look at him. "I don't really drink that anymore. I will have one occasionally."

I open a water bottle for him and hand it to him. "I have to tell you something," he starts, and I just look at him. "Talk is already starting about you and Drew."

"What?" I ask, shocked. "How?" I shake my head; this is what happens in the South. The chatter goes around so fast.

"He was in town this morning with I guess the girl he was with yesterday," he tells me, and I look at him with my mouth hanging open. "Someone told Kallie, and she told me."

"Oh my god," I say, putting my hand to my mouth. "How fucking ..." I start to pace in the kitchen. "How pathetic is this going to make me look?" He watches me as I pace. "My first boyfriend takes off for five years, leaving me without a second look, and the man who I was going to marry is with a new girl five hours later."

"That doesn't make you look pathetic," he says. "It makes us look like idiots."

"What are you talking about?" I shout at him.

"You left Drew," he points out.

"Oh, yeah, 'cause that sounds better. We aren't together because he was fucking another woman because I didn't give it up to him." I close my eyes and put my fingers on the bridge of my nose. "Oh my god. It took them three years to look at me without pity when you left," I say, and I can see him wince.

"No offense, but I used to walk into places, and it used to be, 'Oh, dear, you'll find love soon.' What a fucking asshole."

"If you want, we can head into town now and make out in the middle of Main Street." He smiles at me. "Can you imagine what they'd say?"

"Yeah, I'll be the biggest bitch of all time. It's no wonder she left him. She never got over Ethan." I mock the way the town would talk.

"Did you?" he asks, and I look at him. "Did you get over me?"

I think about my answer. Well, I know my answer, but I'm not sure I'm ready to admit it. "What are you asking me, Ethan?"

"I'm asking if you got over me," he asks point-blank.

"Do I even have to answer this question?" I shake my head. "You heard Drew. I never slept with him, and I was going to marry him."

"That could mean so many things," he says to me. "It could be that you weren't attracted to him. It could be that you weren't ready for it. It could be you were saving yourself for marriage."

"Saving myself for marriage. We slept together five times a week, if not more!" I shout at him, and I want to take it back. I don't want him to know that I still remember. "I think saving myself for marriage was out the door."

"When I would be out on a mission, we sometimes would have to wait it out. During those times was when I used to talk to you the most," he tells me. "In my head, I used to tell you about my day."

"I don't know if I can do this," I say, shaking my head. "I thought I could do it, but I don't know if I can."

"Why?" he asks, crossing his hands over his chest. "Tell me why."

"Because it hurts," I say, the pain in my chest heavy again.

"Because it hurts right here." I point at my chest. "Because those years without you were the worst. Because knowing you were out there without me was unbearable." I wipe the tear away.

"Because you love me," he tells me. "I know you do, Em," he says as he comes around the counter, and I hold my breath. My heart speeds up faster as he cups my face in his hands. "I know because I love you just as much. Thinking about you for the past five years was my own living hell. I thought it was what I deserved for walking away from you.

"Every single birthday, I would watch the sunrise. Every single time I would walk outside, I would look up at the stars and wonder where you were. Every single time my heart beat, it beat for you." His voice goes soft, and his face comes closer. "You can fight it all you want, but you and me, Sunrise, it's a forever kind of love," he says, and his lips find mine in the softest way for just for a moment. "I'm sorry. I shouldn't have taken that kiss. I told myself that I would wait for you to be ready." His hands fall from my face, and my hands come up to touch my lips.

"What if I'm never ready?" I ask, and he looks down.

"Then we are going to be two sad single people for the rest of our lives," he says. "I'm going to head out."

I don't move from my spot in the kitchen as I hear the door close, and then his car starts, and he drives away. I open the oven, taking out the food, and eat by myself at the island. It's not the first time I've eaten alone in this house. I spend most of my meals alone, and I am okay with it. I sit here, playing our talk over and over in my head. I think of Ethan and his talk, and then I think of Drew and his blatant disrespect for me by bringing his girl into town less than twenty-four hours after returning his ring to him.

I slam the fork down and grab my car keys. The minute my foot touches the last step, the clouds open, and the rain pours down. Not just a little drizzle, I'm talking downpour, and by the time I get in my car, I'm soaked all the way through. I don't care as I drive with the wipers going as fast as they can. Yet I can barely see the road. It takes me more time than I thought to get there, and when I get out, I can't avoid being rained on. The sound of thunder now comes rolling in, and when I knock on the door, harder than I wanted to, a bolt of lightning illuminates the sky. I wait at the door as the wind picks up and the water flies at me.

He opens the door, and I see him wearing shorts and nothing else. I had this whole speech prepared, but now, looking at him, all the words are out of my head, so I say the two words that I was going to end the speech with. "Fuck you." He just looks at me, which makes him even hotter. "Fuck you for everything."

He stands there, holding the door with one hand, and I advance and then push him with everything I have. With my hands on his chest, I push him back, and he stumbles back a couple of steps and the wind slams the door behind me. "Fuck you," I say again, pushing him again. "I was getting over you. I was moving on, and then you just come back and ..." I push him, but this time, he grabs my arms. Neither of us says anything as I try to rip my hands free from him. My heart pounds as if I just ran a marathon. My stomach sinks, or maybe it's the butterflies from touching him.

My back is against the door now, and I try to push him away one more time, but this time, he steps in closer to me. The sound of the rain hitting the door echoes in the doorway. He pushes my hands beside my head. I catch my breath from running up here and pushing him back. He looks at me, and I see that he's so close to me, he's too close to me. I look at him in the eyes, look at the blue of his eyes, and I can't believe he's here. In all this time having him here, I never really had to think he was actually here. After five years, he's here in front of me, after years of dreaming of touching him and actually touching him. It's overwhelming, and I do the only thing I can. I lean my head forward, and before you know it, my lips are on his.

He opens his mouth for me and slides his tongue in with mine. I think I moan, or maybe it's him. Either way, he moves in even closer to me, making my head touch the door softly. His fingers intertwine in mine as our tongues wrestle with each other. The sound of our heavy breathing is cut out by the thunder again. He bends his knees a bit and turns his head to the other side, and his hands leave mine as he takes my head in his hand, and my hand slips from his hands to his arms and then his back.

I want to touch him everywhere. I move my hands from his shoulder to his face the same time he holds my face in his hands. I arch my back to get closer to him, and his hand slips around my waist while I move my hand from his face to his neck and then to his shoulders. The whole time, our heads move from side to side to get the kiss to go deeper. His one arm around my waist brings me closer to him, and our heads finally let go just a little as our lips move away from each other. Our noses still touch as I open my eyes and look at him, his lips come closer to mine now, and the hand I had on his neck slowly moves away from him. His hands fall from my waist, and I just look at him. The man who broke my heart five years ago by walking away from me, the man who I tried to get over, the man who I will never stop loving. He takes a step away from me, and I open the door, and it's my turn to walk away from him.

Twenty

ETHAN

I watch her through the rain as she walks to her car. I call out her name, but she ignores me. "Emily!" I shout, walking out of the house into the pouring rain. "Emily!" I shout her name again, and I can see her shoulders shaking. "Emily." I jog to her and stop her from opening the door. "Emily, stop."

"No." She doesn't turn around as her shoulders shake, and I see her head fall forward.

"Sunrise," I say her name, and then the thunder claps. "Please." I put my hands on her arms and pull her to me. Her back to my chest and I wrap my arms around the top of her chest, hoping my heat will get her to stop shaking as the rain just pours all around us.

"I was moving on," she says, sobbing out almost in a wail, and I feel so helpless. There is nothing I can do to make this better, and it's killing me. "I was doing okay." She puts her hand on my arms around her chest. When she showed up, I was shocked. I never thought she would come over on her own. When I left her, so many things were going through my mind. I wanted to tell her that I would spend the rest of my life making sure she is okay. I wanted to tell her that from this moment forward, I would never leave her again. But I needed to go slow. At least that is what I thought.

"Sunrise, I love you," I whisper in her ear, and she stops shaking. "I have loved you my whole life. I will love you in this life, and I'm sure that I loved you in a past life, and I'll find you in the next life. You are the reason I'm alive today."

"You left me," she says the three words that cut me. "You just left me." She turns in my arms now. "You left me, and I had to learn how to breathe without my chest hurting. I had to learn how to go an hour without wanting to call you. I had to learn how to wake up and pretend I was okay. I had to learn how to live again." She puts her head down and cries, and I pull her into my arms. "I can't survive that again."

"You don't have to. You won't ever have to," I say. "Let me prove it to you," I beg her. I will spend my whole life begging her. "You deserve so much better than me," I admit. "You deserve someone who doesn't make you cry. You deserve a man who lifts you up instead of pulling you down. You deserve a man who has never hurt you. You deserve a man who doesn't have you doubting your worth because you are worth everything. You deserve all of that." My heart breaks. "I should let you find it, but I'm not that good of a man. I am going to prove to you that I deserve it." I put my hand under her chin to lift her face up to see me. "There is nothing more in this life I need to do but prove it to you."

"What if you realize that you aren't in love with me?" she asks the question I've asked myself over and over again. One of my biggest fears is that she realized she never really loved me.

"How could I not love you?" I say and then take her hand and place it over my heart. "You come into the room, and my heart feels so big it might come out of my chest. I look over at you, and my heart races. Emily, you are my heart." I put my forehead on hers.

"You are going to have to give me time," she says. "I just …"

"I will give you all the time you need," I say softly. Taking her face in my hands, I rub her cheeks with my thumbs. "I love you."

"Ethan." She says my name, and the rains starts to slow down. "I beg you." Her voice goes low. "Don't do this if you aren't sure."

"You are my reason," I say. "You are the reason that I get up in the morning. You are the reason I fought to live. You. Are. My. Reason."

Her hands come up to hold my hands on her face, and she whispers the words I've heard her say in my dreams for five years. "I love you, Ethan." She laughs now as she cries at the same time. "I never stopped. I tried, I really did, and it just … A part of me knew I would love you always."

"Sunrise," I say as my own tears stream down my face. "I'm about to break a promise to you, and I really don't want to do it."

"Kiss me, Ethan." She doesn't even finish saying the words before my mouth is on hers, and we are clinging to each other. This right here is the reason I survived what I did. This kiss, this love, this woman is my reason for everything.

She pulls away first. "I have to go and get things ready for tomorrow." She looks down. "Can we keep this our secret for now?" She must see the hurt on my face. "Not because I'm unsure or anything. I just want it to be ours for a while."

"I'll do whatever you want to do," I say, and I'm honest about it. "Until I snap. Because if I want to kiss you, I'm going to kiss you."

She rolls her eyes. "Well, I see that didn't change."

"I'm the same man you fell in love with," I say. "I just have a few broken pieces."

"So do I," she says, and I kiss her again.

"Will you call me when you get home?" I ask, not wanting her to go. I want her to stay and spend the night.

"I don't have your number," she tells me, and I smile.

"It's the same as my old one. Casey kept paying the plan the whole time." I smile at her.

"Okay," she whispers and leans in, giving me another kiss. "I'll call you when I get home."

I open the door for her, and she gets in, looking at me. "I can't believe this is happening," she says. "This, me and you."

"It never stopped," I say, closing the door and watching her drive away. My heart hurt just a touch that she didn't stay. I walk back into the house, my step a tad lighter than it was before. She calls me when she gets home, and we spend an hour talking about Drew and him showing off the new girl. When I hang up with her, it's to me telling her I love her.

The next morning, I'm parked in front of her school, and I see her getting out of her car and making her way over. Her hair is perfectly styled as she wears another skirt with a nice top. Her bags are in one hand and her coffee in the other hand. I take my phone and call her, and I see her smile and then answer me.

"Hello," she says.

"I love when you smile," I say, and she stops walking. "You look beautiful this morning." Her head flies up, and she looks around.

"Where are you?" she asks. I get out of my truck, and she sees me. "What are you doing here?" she asks into the phone, but then I'm close enough to her. I hang up as I walk over and bend down. I see her eyes in a panic, but I do it anyway. I kiss her on her cheek.

"I took Amelia and Chelsea to breakfast this morning," I

say, and she smiles. "I missed a lot while I was gone, so I'm catching up."

"Well, isn't that the sweetest," she says, and a couple of the kids say hello to her when they walk in, and the bell rings. "I have to get going, but ..."

"Why don't you come over after school and we can make dinner?" I suggest, and she looks down. "Or not."

"How about you come over to my place," she tells me. "I have some work to do, and I work better at my house."

"Done," I say, and I look around, seeing that some eyes are on us. "I really want to kiss you right now."

She smiles shyly. "If it makes you feel better, I really want you to kiss me, too." Another bell rings. "I have to go."

"See you later, Sunrise," I say softly, and she walks away from me. Chelsea and Amelia wait for her by the door and say something to her, and then the three of them laugh.

I get into my truck and make my way over to my next stop. I look at the house and see two American flags by the door. I walk up the steps and open the door, seeing Cassandra sitting behind the desk. "I heard the ruffling of feathers that you were in town," she says, getting up and walking around her desk.

"Hey there," I say, bending to give her a hug. She's been working for Beau for the past fifteen years. "Is he in?"

"He sure is." She smiles. "Do you want me to bring you anything to drink?" she asks. I just shake my head and walk over, knocking on the doorframe. He's sitting behind his desk, reading something, and he looks up.

He doesn't smile at me nor does he have any reaction to me standing here. "I was wondering if we can talk?" I ask, my hands getting clammy with nerves. He stands up now walking around the desk, and he leans on it. Looking around the office, I see that it looks almost the same. There is a new couch and some new pictures that line the wall, but in the middle is the picture of my mother and him on their wedding day with me standing in front of them.

"I," I start to say, and I look down. "I wanted to come by and talk to you."

"Well, here I am," he says, folding his arms over his chest.

"I get that you're pissed at me," I say, sitting down on the couch.

"Oh, I'm not pissed at you," he says, pushing off now and coming over to sit on the opposite couch, facing me. "I'm disappointed, not pissed." He leans back. "Okay, fine, I'm a bit pissed off also."

"And you have every right to be." I lean forward, putting my elbows on my knees.

"Do you know I found out in this office?" he tells me, and I look at him, shocked. "The day I became mayor, I came in here and was sneaking a drink of your grandfather's whiskey. I opened the locked drawer, not thinking anything of it." My heart beats so fast. "There it was, a paper telling me that the woman I loved had a baby with my brother."

"Oh my god," I whisper, and he just looks at me.

"I've loved your mother my whole life. Every single day from the moment I can form memories, she was the one I was going to marry, and there it was that she chose someone else and not me."

"What did you do?" I ask, feeling a sudden pain for him.

"I did what you did, more or less. I said not nice things. Things that to this day, I thank god she forgave me for. But when I heard her story, and I heard the reasons, I was so fucking relieved she didn't give my brother you because you are hands down the best thing that will ever happen to him." I wipe away the tear from my eye. "You said things that I know you regret, trust me, I know that, but you hurt a lot of people by staying away."

"I know," I say. "I just ..."

"Your father," he starts. "Jacob." When he says his name, I want to tell him that his name is dad. He's my dad. "He gave up everything for you." He shakes his head. "And I mean everything. He gave up the woman he loved and the life he wanted, and he did it without once looking back. He didn't care what blood type you were. None of us did."

"It was a shock," I say. "I felt like my whole life was just a farce. I was scared, Uncle Beau," I finally tell him, my voice going low. "I was scared that I would be just like him. That I would turn out like him." I cry now. "Fuck, he threw me away." He gets up now, coming over to me, and puts his arm around my shoulder.

"He didn't throw you away," he says. Whispering, he squeezes me, "He gave you the best gift he could have given you. He gave you Jacob."

"I know," I say. "I know that now."

"My father was not a nice person. My brother was just as stupid, who had no balls to stand up to him. He dropped your mother without thinking twice about you." I put my hands in front of my face. "He's not a man, he's a coward, and you were raised better than that."

"I was," I say. "It's why I came back."

"You being gone hurt everyone in a different way," he tells me. "It hurt not to be able to watch you grow to be the man you are. It hurt not to be there when you had doubts and thought you had no one to turn to. It hurt watching your mother miss a piece of her. It hurt watching your father not be able to make sure you were okay. He had to wait for Casey to give him whatever news he had. It would take a toll on him after he did find out," he tells me. "He would get quiet for a couple of weeks. I don't know how he did it." He shakes his head. "Knowing that your kid is out there but not being able to talk to them and hold them." My heart breaks for my father. I never thought about what this was doing to him.

"I was a selfish asshole who only thought about myself," I say, wiping my eye.

"You weren't a selfish asshole," he tells me. "You were a man finding his path."

"Well, this path led me to the one place I need to be," I say. "Home."

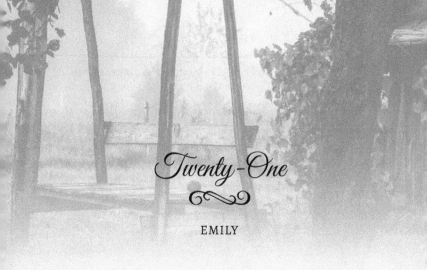

Twenty-One

EMILY

"If you guys need any extra help, all you have to do is let me know," I say to the kids as they start to walk out. "I'm here early in the morning and during all of lunch."

I sit down at the desk and start to pile up the things I need to bring home to correct, and when I walk out of the classroom, I see the halls are pretty much empty. A couple of students stand at their lockers, trying to clean it out before the last day of school. It's always a bittersweet time of year when the kids get ready to leave. Some of the kids that I've taught for the past three years are graduating, and I'm going to miss them. I get into the car and make my way home, with the window open and the air blowing through my hair.

I pull up, and I'm shocked to see Ethan there sitting on the porch. He gets up when he sees my car, opening the door as soon as I put it in park. "Hey," I say right before he leans in and kisses me on the lips.

My hand comes up to hold his cheek. "Hi," he says, smiling, and I lean forward for another kiss. "Hi." He steps out of the car and holds his hand out for me. I grab his hand, getting out. He opens the back door, grabbing my bag, and we walk up the steps to the front door.

"Were you waiting long?" I ask, opening the door and feeling the cool air hit me right away. I walk in and go straight to the fridge, grabbing him a water bottle. He sits on the stool after putting my stuff on the couch. "Here." I hand him the bottle, and he finishes it. "I wish I knew you were coming. I would have given you the garage code." As soon as I say the words, I want to take it back. Maybe he won't remember. "It's 1-7-1-4," I say, and the look on his face tells me that he remembers. He gets up, coming around the counter toward me. "Ethan," I say as he picks me up and sets me on the counter.

"That's the first day I told you I loved you," he tells me in almost a whisper.

"You remembered." He puts his hands beside my hips, coming in and rubbing his nose against mine.

"I remember everything when it comes to you," he says softly. "Every single moment, every single day, every single memory is engraved inside me." His voice is so low that if I wasn't this close I would not hear it. He kisses me softly. Then his tongue comes out to lick my lower lip, and my tongue comes out to meet his. He kisses me, and I suddenly hate that I'm wearing a skirt and can't wrap my legs around him. His hands come up, one holding my neck while the other pushes my hair away from my face, and he holds it in his hand. The sound of us kissing fills the room, and just when I'm about to wrap my legs around him anyway, a knock breaks us up. "Were you expecting anyone?" he asks, his chest rising and falling. His lips wet from my kiss.

"No," I say. Pushing him away, I hop down, walking to the front door as another knock sounds. I open the door, and I'm shocked that it's Olivia and Kallie. "Hey," I say, smiling.

"Sorry to just drop in," Olivia says, and then she looks

behind me, and I know right away that they must see him because they both look at me with their mouth open. They recover pretty quickly, and I see a smirk form on Olivia's face while Kallie smiles so big. "We didn't mean to interrupt anything."

"Don't be silly," I say, and then I feel him at my back, his hands on my shoulders. "Come in."

I move aside, and Kallie comes in, getting on her tippy toes to give Ethan a hug. He hugs her around her shoulders and turns to walk into the house with her beside him. "We are going to be five minutes max," Olivia tells me, and I just shake my head, walking into the house. I come to a stop when I see Kallie sitting on a stool with Ethan getting water out of the fridge for her.

I try not to make it seem like I'm thrown for a loop as Olivia tells me about all the details with the carnival Saturday, and when they leave five minutes later, he looks over at me. "What's wrong?" he asks, and I avoid his look.

"Nothing," I say. "It's nothing."

"Sunrise," he says, and I look at him, and I'm annoyed now that even after five years of being apart from him, he still knows me.

"I bought this house for you," I say finally, and he stands in the kitchen, shocked. "I know it's stupid, and I had to literally beg your mother to sell it to me, but when I told her that I wanted to make you a home for when you came back, she gave in. I wonder if she did it because she felt sorry for me. Still holding out with the hope that you would come back." I wipe a tear away. "But now having you here in the kitchen, and it's just, it was always meant to be yours."

"It was meant to be ours," he says now. "My mother was holding on to this house as a wedding present." It's my turn now to be shocked. "So, in the end, it was always meant to be ours." He smiles. "Go get changed, and I'll start on dinner."

I don't say anything else. Instead, I walk into my bedroom and slip on a pair of shorts and a tank top. When I come out of the bedroom, he's already in the kitchen cooking. I slip onto the stool, and I know I'm supposed to do work, but I can't. Instead, I sit and watch him. "You still like steak, right?" he asks, taking the steak out of the freezer, and I nod. He pours me a glass of wine, and when he brings it to me, he kisses my lips softly.

Dinner is made with small talk. He tells me about meeting with Beau, and he talks about the work he is doing at the barn. When it's time to clean up, I look at him. "You cook, I clean." I lean down now and kiss him. "You know the rules."

I clean up, and when I'm done, he comes over and grabs my hand, leading me outside to the hammock. He lies on his back and holds out his hand. "Lie with me," he says, and I get in with him. With my head on his shoulder and my leg over his, we look up at the stars. "I used to do this," he starts. "Every night, I used to go out and look at the stars and tell you about my day."

I look up at him, and he leans down and kisses me. He spends the night telling me about the friends he's made and the house he has in the woods. He kisses me every single time he finishes a sentence, and both of us fall asleep swaying in the hammock. When the sun comes up, we watch it together with his arms around me. I get out, then hold out my hand for him, and when we walk into the house, I make him coffee. He finishes his cup and then kisses me until my knees go weak as he leaves. "Tonight, let's hit up the diner."

"That's a bold move," I say.

"I want to take you out," he tells me. "But we can wait until next week."

"Are you going straight to the barn?" I ask, and he shakes his head.

"I have to get my change of clothes," he tells me, and I take a big step with my next words.

"Why don't you pack it in your truck in case …?" I don't say the rest, and he smiles. "I'll see you later."

"Oh, you can bet on that, Sunrise," he says, kissing me one last time and walking out.

My day goes by so fast I don't even have time to eat lunch, and when I'm getting into my car, I'm shocked when I see a red rose on my seat with a note.

I can't wait to see more sunrises with you.

E

I bring the rose to my nose and make my way home. I don't see his truck there, and when I walk into the house, I have to stop when I see rose petals all over the floor. My bag slips out of my hands as I walk into the house, and there are roses everywhere. "What the …" I say. Looking around, I walk to the big bouquet with a card. Seeing my name in Ethan's handwriting on the front, I try to see through the tears.

To my love on her birthday. I have so much to make up for, but the biggest for me is missing your birthdays. Happy Birthday to the woman who gives me life, to the woman who makes living easy. Whose smile brightens up the room.

I love you with all that I am.

E

I bring the card to my chest and cry, and just like that, I feel his arms around me. "Happy Birthday, Sunrise." I turn in his arms and cry in his chest. "I didn't want you to cry," he says, kissing my head.

"Then stop doing romantic shit," I say through my tears as he laughs.

"I picked up some food," he tells me, but I look up at him as he wipes away the tears from my face. "I got your favorite," he says. "I mean, I had to text Jenna to make sure it was still your favorite." I laugh when he says this.

"Where is it?" I ask.

"In the oven," he says, and I look down.

"You know what I missed most about you?" I ask, and he smiles. "The way you kiss me." He bends and kisses me softly on the lips. I step out of his grasp, and I hold his hand, bringing him to the couch. "If we are celebrating my birthday, then I want to do it with you and me making out on the couch." He smiles at me, and I can see that he's just as into me as he was all those years ago. I sit on the couch, and he just shakes his head.

"If we are going to make out on the couch ..." He pulls me up to stand and turns me around. "We are going to do it like we always did it." He lies on the couch and pulls me on top of him, and I feel every single muscle he has.

"Oh, I like this a lot more than my idea," I say, laughing. He captures my mouth, and we kiss until the both of us are literally coming out of our skin. "Will you stay the night with me?"

"Are you sure?" he asks, and I just look at him.

"It's a birthday ritual," I remind him, and both of us just look into each other's eyes. The last time we celebrated his birthday before he left, he did it sliding into me at midnight.

"Sunrise," he asks, "are you sure?"

"No," I tell him honestly. "I'm afraid," I tell him, getting up and looking at him. He sits now. "I'm afraid of tomorrow. I'm afraid I'm going to wake up, and you'll be gone. I'm afraid that one of these days, I'll come home, and you'll be gone. I'm afraid that my love isn't going to be enough to keep you here." I give him all my fears. "I'm so afraid that I won't survive this again." I sob out. "I know I told myself not to get my hopes high. I told myself that I wasn't going to count on you being here, but I have all the broken pieces that somehow glued together, just not complete."

He gets up now. "I'm going to spend the rest of my life

making sure that you know I'm not going anywhere." He kisses my hands. "Knowing that you have this fear breaks me. I want to put all your pieces back together again. Let me be your glue." He kisses me. "Let me be the one who puts you together again." I don't have to answer him because he picks me up and carries me to my bedroom, holding me the whole time.

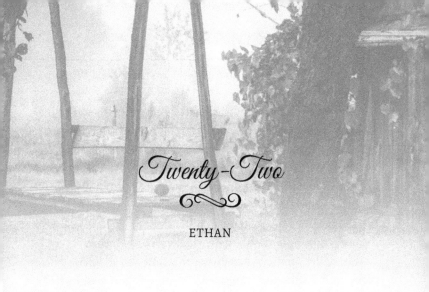

Twenty-Two

ETHAN

"Why are you crying?" I ask when she walks into the house on the last day of school. I walk to her and take her in my arms as she quietly sobs. "Sunrise," I say, kissing her head. I had just finished in the shower when she walked in. Slowly, over the past four days, I've been leaving a lot more of my things here. I don't have much stuff anyway, but most of it is here now.

"I'm going to miss them so much," she says, and I get it now. It was the last day of school for her, and half of the students that she teaches are graduating. It's been four days since we've woken up together, four days that I've made her dinner every single night. Four days of surprising her with a birthday surprise.

"It's going to be okay," I say. "You get to see them all tomorrow at the carnival."

"What is going on here?" She finally looks around and notices all the balloons all over the place. "It's the fourth birthday I missed." She puts her hands to her mouth as she looks around, seeing a hundred balloons that I had delivered.

"Oh my god," she says, seeing the box on the table. "What in the world?"

"This is your fourth birthday gift," I say when she walks to the table. I wrapped it with white wrapping paper, and there is a big pink bow on it. "Open it." I smile at her, and she just looks at me. Her blue eyes light up now so much that I have no choice but to lean over and kiss her neck. She waits for me to stop kissing her before slipping the bow off and ripping open the paper. The box she gave me not too long ago sits in front of her. She looks at the box, knowing it's hers and then looks at me. "Open it."

She slides open the box except this time, it's different. She picks up the shirt and brings it to her nose. "You washed it?" She laughs and cries at the same time. "I haven't washed this in five years."

"I know," I say, and she throws her head back, laughing while she holds the shirt to her chest.

She puts the shirt down next to the box and takes out the first frame with a picture of us on the beach. "You put it in a frame." She smiles through the tears, and then she takes the other one out. "You put them all in a frame."

"I did," I say. "I thought we could put them up around the house instead of keeping them in a box."

She puts the picture down and then walks away to her bedroom, and I stand here in the kitchen waiting for her. She comes back with another frame, and I smile at her. It's the picture I've kept in my wallet the whole time. "This one I want to keep by the bed." She shows me. "And this one." She picks up the one of both of us on the beach. "This should go on the mantel."

"I like that," I say, and that night, she cooks side by side with me. It takes longer than it should, but every time she comes close to me, I have to stop and kiss her. I often wake in the middle of the night, afraid I'm going to have a nightmare and scare her. When I see her lying there, I just have to touch her.

That night, we slip into bed, and I get lost in her, her kisses, her touch, everything about her. We've been good about going slow, and I refuse to push her. She'll have to be the one to take that next step.

I'm making her tea the next morning when she slips her arms around my waist and kisses my back. "Good morning," she mumbles. "When did you get up?"

"About an hour ago," I say, looking at the clock. "I was just coming to wake you. What time do we need to be at the carnival?"

"In about an hour," she says, going to the counter. "There are so many balloons," she says, looking around. We carry our drinks outside and sit watching nothing, her feet in my lap. "How do you want to handle this?" She takes a sip of her tea and looks at me.

"What do you mean?" I ask.

"Us at the carnival." Her eyes are on me. "Like, are we going to tell people we're a couple, or do we keep it to ourselves?"

"If it was up to me, everyone would already know," I say. "I don't have anything to hide."

"I don't have anything to hide either, but," she says, and my stomach drops, "I was just engaged and ..."

"He's dating someone else," I say, "and he's been seen with her more than once."

"I know, but just because he's like that doesn't mean I have to be like that," she says. It bugs the shit out of me that she doesn't want people to know we are together, but I have to respect her. I don't say anything to her, the conversation just stops, and when I slip on my blue jeans and gray shirt, I run my hands through my hair, and for the first time, it feels long.

I walk out of the bedroom just in time to see her in blue cutoffs and a gray shirt tied at the waist.

"You ready?" I ask, and she slips on her white sneakers while I do the same. "Do you want me to meet you there, or do you want to take one car?"

"I know that you're angry," she says, standing and looks at me. "And I get it. But ..."

"But nothing, Emily," I say. I'm not angry, and I'm not mad. I'm disappointed, but I also know she is the one who is going to decide what happens in this relationship. I lost that right when I left. "I'll just meet you there. That way, no one says anything." I turn to walk out the door and feel like an asshole, but I'm stubborn enough not to turn around and go back to see if she is okay. Instead, I wait in my truck, seeing her come out with her head down as she walks to her car. She takes off without saying anything to me, and I drive right behind her, and when we pull up to the carnival, I'm shocked. This looks like the state fair and not just a school carnival. I get out of the truck and look over to see that she is already walking in. "Fuck," I say under my breath, and before I can chase after her, I'm joined by Quinn, Keith, Toby, and Reed. "Boys," I say to them, and they all smile at me. "This is insane."

"Have you known my mother to do anything normal?" Reed says, and I just shake my head. "There are legit carnival games where you can win stuffed animals."

"You know that this is the state fair, right?" Quinn says. "She called and begged them to come this weekend and paid for it."

"I don't even have a car," Toby says. "I'm going to go and see if I can get Laura to ride the Ferris wheel with me." He walks away to the group of girls that are waiting at the ticket booth.

We walk through the fair, and Reed was right. Olivia blew this shit up. There are so many people here that it's hard to walk. I spot Beau and my mother walking along, hugging them both, and it bothers me that I'm not with Emily. It bothers me so much that I walk around the whole place looking for her. I finally catch her with her students, and she laughs at something one of them said.

I watch her, my chest full of love, and just as I knew she would, she feels me staring at her and turns to look around and spots me. She raises her hand this time and calls me over. I walk over to her. "Have fun, girls," she tells them and then turns to walk my way. "Where have you been?"

"Around," I say, wanting nothing more than to kiss her lips like I do at home.

"I'm sorry," she says softly, and the wind comes now blowing her hair everywhere, and she turns to take it away from her face. "I didn't know how to handle all of this. I let my fear get to me."

"It's okay," I say, looking down myself. "I'm sorry for taking off and being a giant ass."

She smiles and looks down now. "Do you want to walk with me?" she asks shyly, and I just smile.

"Lead the way," I say, and she turns to walk. I walk next to her. "Did you go on any rides?" I ask, and she shakes her head. I'm about to ask her to go on a ride when I feel her fingers graze mine. I try not to think too much of it, but then her fingers slip in mine, and I look down at them.

"Are you sure?" I say with her hand in mine.

"I'm sure that I want to hold your hand," she tells me. "I'm sure that my day will be better with you by my side." She looks up, and it's as if the seas part because when we both look up, we see Drew.

I'm expecting her to let my hand go, but she doesn't, and it could be that she's in shock. He's there at the fair with a woman standing next to him, holding his hand. That isn't what gets us, though. What shocks us, or maybe just me, is the little bump that the lady is definitely carrying. "Oh my god," I mumble, trying to turn us the other way. Instead, we come face-to-face with them, and I know that eyes are on us. I take one look around to see that, but it also takes me that one look around to see my family closes in on us—Mom and Beau to the left, Casey and Olivia to the right. Standing right behind Drew and his girl are my father and Kallie. All my sisters and brothers are lingering close by, too.

"Well," Drew says, smiling, and I want nothing more than to throat punch him. "Fancy meeting you guys here."

"Fancy, my ass," I say, laughing. "You knew she was going to be here."

He looks at our joined hands. "Wow, that didn't take you long," he says, bitterly pointing at our hands.

"You can't be serious right now," Emily hisses, and I look over at the girl. She's the total opposite of Emily. Her hair is bleached blond. Her fake eyelashes are on so thick I can't even see her eyes. She wears a tight one-piece skirt with a flannel shirt tied under her belly.

"It's a great turnout." Drew ignores my question and then turns to his girl. "Baby," he says, "this is Emily and Ethan." The girl has no idea who we are, and I have to shake my head. "Guys, this is Mandie."

"It's nice to meet you." She smiles at us and then looks at him.

"It's good to put a face to the voice," Emily says from beside me, and Mandie looks confused. "How long have you guys been together?" she asks her.

Mandie is quick to answer. "Almost eighteen months."

At the same time, Drew says, "A couple of weeks."

"Eighteen months!" Emily shouts out a bit too loud, and whoever wasn't looking at this scene unfold is now looking. "Wow, definitely dodged that bullet." She laughs and turns to me, then looks back and sees Mandie all confused.

"We were engaged," she tells her. "Broke it off when he pocket dialed me banging you in the car." I roll my lips when I see Drew turn red, and Mandie puts her hand on her stomach. "Well, if you'll excuse us." She looks up at me. "I'm in the mood for a funnel cake."

I smile at her, being so brave and not letting this get to her. Knowing that everyone is watching, she is powering through. "Let's go get you a funnel cake," I say and then look at Drew and Mandie. "Congratulations on the baby." I turn and walk away from them, and when I look over at her, she's smiling. "Are you okay?" I ask almost in a whisper.

"I'm shocked," she says honestly, then stops and looks at me. The noise of people talking is all around us. "I'm not going to lie. Fuck eighteen months." She shakes her head. "He's having a baby with someone. How was that going to work?"

"I have no idea," I say, and she looks down and then up again. "We can go if you want."

"Um, I want a funnel cake," she says. "Then I want to ride the Ferris wheel." She steps in a touch closer. "Where we can make out like we did the first time." I smile at her, and she looks around. "Then you are going to win me a bear because that is what I want, and after that, I'm going home, and I'm going to unwrap my fifth birthday gift." She winks at me.

"Sunrise," I say. "I didn't get you anything for your fifth birthday gift. I was going to ..." I start to say, but she puts her finger over my mouth to stop me from talking.

She gets on her tippy toes. "You're my present." She tilts her head just a bit. "Now, give me a kiss and get me a funnel cake." I don't wait a second more before I push her hair away from her face and kiss her, letting everyone know I'm back, and she's mine.

Twenty-Three

EMILY

He kisses me, and I don't even care. When he left the house, it hurt that I hurt him. I didn't want him to ever feel like he didn't mean anything to me or that we didn't matter, so walking the carnival without him felt wrong. I kept looking for him, and finally when I saw him, I knew that I didn't care what anyone said. All I knew is that I wanted him beside me.

I called him over, not thinking anything, and when I saw Drew with his girlfriend, who was pregnant, I waited for the hurt to hit me. I waited for my chest to feel tight, and the tears to come, but none of that happened, and I finally admitted to myself that I never really loved him like that. I walked away, holding Ethan's hand, and I knew that the next step would be mine to make. I knew he was waiting for the green light, and it was time. I wanted all of him. I wanted to give him all of me.

"You taste like sugar," he says softly against my lips. "You had a funnel cake already."

"I did," I admit. "But I wanted another one, and I wanted it with you."

"I love you," he says to me and turns to order me a funnel

cake. Handing it to me, he grabs some napkins. We walk away and come face-to-face with most of his family. "Hey," he says, looking around. "Thank you, guys," he says now, and I look over at him, confused. "You guys saw what was going down, and you had my back."

"Always," Beau says to him, slapping him on the shoulder. "Now, does this mean you two are back together?"

"It means that I want her, and luckily for me, she wants me back," he says, grabbing me around my shoulders. "Now if you all will excuse me, my girl wants to make out with me on the Ferris wheel."

"That's so gross," Chelsea says while Amelia scrunches up her nose.

We walk away from them, and we get on the Ferris wheel. "Are you sure that you're okay?" he asks when the wheel starts turning.

"I didn't love him," I admit. "Like I loved him as a person, but ..." I don't say anything else when I feel him put his arm around me, and his thumb rubs my arm up and down. "It's you." I look at him. "It's always just been you." I lean in and kiss him, my tongue sliding with his as he holds my face with his free hand.

We make out like a couple of teenagers, and when we get off the Ferris wheel, he walks over to a booth that has teddy bears. He wins me the teddy bear on the first try, too. I don't know why I'm surprised, but when he hands it to me, I squeal and hug it to my chest. We walk around the fair holding hands. No one looks at us, and no one points at us. We're just Emily and Ethan. He stops when he sees his brothers, and they challenge him to a shooting game. I just shake my head and watch him do his thing. The sun goes down, and the lights come on, and it's just magical. It's honestly the best day ever when he turns around and tosses me another bear while his brother asks for a rematch.

Seeing him rebuilding that bond he had with them so long ago makes it so much more. Knowing how far he's come, I could not love him more. When we walk out of the carnival, he looks at me. "Are we leaving your car here or mine?"

"Why are we leaving any of the cars here?" I ask, and he looks around. "Amelia!" he calls out to his sister. "How did you get here?"

"Mom and Dad," she says, and he grabs my keys. "Take Emily's car home. We'll pick it up later."

She laughs. "Later or tomorrow?"

"Monday." He winks at her, then grabs my hand and drags me away from her.

"Oh my god," I say, laughing, looking over at Amelia cringing. He gets me in the truck, and before I can even say anything, he is racing out of the parking lot. I laugh so hard when I look over at him. "Five years, Sunrise," he says, and I lean over and kiss his neck, sucking in a little bit. He groans, and I smile, knowing he can't do anything because he's driving.

"All week," I tell him, whispering in his ear and then licking his lobe. "Lying by you, all I wanted to do was jump you." My hand falls to his lap, and I cup his cock.

"Sunrise," he hisses out between clenched teeth. "I am on the edge right now."

"Why?" I ask, sucking in his lobe. "I want you," I say, and I'm about to say something else when the truck comes to a stop. He's out of his seat before I can look around. My door is ripped open, and he picks me up like a rag doll. My legs wrap around his waist as his mouth finds mine. His tongue fights with mine as he walks up to the front door. My hands are already ripping off his shirt as he pushes me into the door and attacks my neck. My back arches, and I hope to fuck he rips off my shirt soon. "Ethan," I say his name as he attacks my neck.

His hand flies to my waist as my shirt rises, and I feel his hands on my body. Five years ago, they were soft. This time, they are rougher, and I need him to touch all of me. I don't know how he does it, but the door opens, and we are inside. He walks straight to my bedroom and tosses me on the bed. I get up on my elbows in time to see him reach behind his head and pull his shirt over his head. At the same time, he kicks off his shoes.

"Last chance," he says. I sit up, reaching out to unsnap his button. Taking off my shirt, I toss it with his discarded one, then kick off my shoes with his.

"I hope that answers your question," I say, and his eyes change as he looks at me in my gray lacy bra.

"I pictured this moment," he tells me, sliding his finger under my bra strap. "Every day." He peels the strap off my shoulder. Leaning down, he moves the cup aside and takes my nipple into his mouth. I close my eyes as he rolls his tongue around and then he bites down like he knows I like it. My hand goes to his head as I moan out. "Fuck, still as responsive as the first time," he says, going to the other side and pushing the cup aside to take the other nipple in his mouth.

I use my right hand to cup his cock, and slowly, he stands up. I bring him to me, and my fingers slowly trace his scar on the side. I lean in and kiss his scar. "I love you," I say and then place my hands on his hips.

I slip his boxers down, and I don't wait any longer to take his cock in my mouth. His hands go into my hair as my tongue swirls around the head of his cock. My hand grips the base of his cock, and I work him with my mouth and my hand. I know that it's only a matter of time before he takes over, just like always. When I take him all the way to the base, his hands grip my hair tighter, and I feel him pulling back, pulling it just enough, and I want to close my legs and grind on him. "Enough." He pushes me back onto the bed, and in one single move, my shorts are ripped off me, and his mouth is on my pussy. He doesn't even move the panties yet; he just licks up in one long lick. "Fuck," he says as he pushes my panties to the side, and his tongue finally flicks my clit.

"Ethan," I say with my eyes closed, opening my legs as much as they can go. We always had the best sex, always. We were never shy in the bedroom. If we wanted to try something, we did, and it always rocked our world. "Right there," I say as he fucks me with two fingers that he slipped in. "Rub right there," I say again as his fingers rub my G-spot, and my hand comes up to play with my nipples.

"I need," I say, panting. "I need ..." I can taste the fall; he bites down on my clit, and right when I start to come, he pulls his mouth away. I groan in frustration, and my eyes are about to open when I feel him slam into me in one hard thrust, causing us both to moan. I look down at his cock as it goes in and out of me in small, hard thrusts. His thick, meaty thighs hit my ass with each thrust. I can't stop watching his cock as my pussy takes all of him. I feel so full, and the sound of us panting fills the room.

"Harder," I say, wanting him to fuck me so hard that I won't be able to walk tomorrow. He slams into me, and I moan and arch my back. "Again," I say as he thrusts into me harder and harder. He takes one hand and pinches my nipple, sending lightning all the way down to my pussy, and he knows it.

"Squeeze me," he says, pinching it and then rolling it between his fingers. I lick my middle finger, and he watches me, his eyes fixated on my finger. "Play with yourself while I fuck you." He doesn't have to tell me twice. My finger rubs my clit side to side.

"Fuck, you're so tight," he says between clenched teeth. "Look at us," he says, looking down at where we meet. "So wet," he says, and I know that I'm getting wetter and wetter as he rubs my G-spot over and over again. "Fuck, I'm almost there," he says, pinching my nipple so much harder now it makes my hand move on my clit frantically.

"That's it, Sunrise," he says. "Come on my cock," he says, and I just listen to him as I come all over his cock. Over and over again, my pussy convulses on his cock. Just when I think I'm coming down from it, he slams into me two more times, and I'm moaning out his name as I come again. He plants himself balls deep in me and comes with a roar. He collapses on top of me, resting his face on my chest.

My legs wrap around his waist as I catch my breath. I close my eyes for just a minute, and then I feel his tongue on my nipples, and my legs tighten around his waist. "Unless you are ready for round two, I suggest you stop that." Instead of moving his mouth away from me, he slips out and then slowly slides back in.

"Time for round two," he says right before he fucks me again until I see stars.

Twenty-Four

ETHAN

"If you keep touching me like that, nothing is going to get done," she says, standing in front of the kitchen sink. She wears my shirt and nothing else while my hands are on her tits, teasing her nipples. "Seriously, Ethan," she moans and pushes her ass back into my cock.

"I miss you," I say into her neck, and she moves to give me access to it.

"You were in me less than five minutes ago." She laughs.

"It's not my fault," I say, and it isn't. I came out of the bedroom, and she was making coffee for me, and she leaned up to reach into the cabinet. Her shirt rose, showing me the bottom of her ass, and well ... I walked up to her, grabbed her by the hips, and lifted her up enough to slide my cock into her. She didn't say a word. She just lay forward on the counter and fucked me back.

"I see you, and I lose control. Are you sore?" I ask. I've taken her over and over again, the both of us always wanting a piece of the other one. The sex between us was always out of this world. She was never shy about it, and when she wanted something, she asked for it. Fuck, she bought the Kama Sutra book one Valentine's Day, and we were working our way through it.

"You asked me if I was sore when we took a bath," she reminds me, looking at me. "While you sat me on the edge and played with me." I smirk, remembering that between eating her and finger fucking her, she was a mess. She finally had enough and just sank on my cock. The water went everywhere, and I mean everywhere. "Go make us something to eat, and then we can continue this," she says. "There is still the couch we have to bless and maybe tonight the hammock."

"Definitely fucking you on the hammock tonight," I say, walking away from her to my cock's strong disapproval. I take out some bacon and eggs while she makes toast, and fifteen minutes later, we are both sitting down eating.

"We should talk about a couple of things," she says, chewing and then taking a sip of her tea. I look over at her. She sits there with her long legs crossed and her hair piled on her head. She has little dots on her neck and around her lips from my beard, and I'm sure there is a hickey on her left thigh. I know I left teeth marks on her left breast when she was riding me.

"What do you want to talk about?" I ask, eating a piece of bacon.

"We've had unprotected sex," she tells me, looking down.

"Yeah." I look over at her. "It's not the first time. I haven't been with anyone."

"I know that," she says. "It's just, I'm not on the pill."

"Okay, and ...?" I look at her.

"Well, we've had sex a lot, and well, I'm not covered. I don't know if you know how babies are made, but ..." She moves her head back and forth.

"I still don't understand what you're trying to say," I say. She drops her fork and gets up, walking to the fridge.

"I'm saying we've had unprotected sex, Ethan. Like, not a

oops one time." She grabs the water bottle and drinks it. "I could get pregnant." She puts her hands on the counter in front of me.

"Okay." I shrug my shoulders. "I mean, we are going to have kids anyway."

"What?" she whispers.

"Sunrise," I say to her while I chew a piece of toast. "We are going to have kids. We always wanted kids, so if it happens now, it happens."

"That's it?" she says, folding her arms. "Just I get pregnant, and that's it. You'll be fine with it."

"Um, yeah," I say. "Why? Would you not be okay with having my baby?"

She glares at me. "I didn't say that. I was just saying that maybe we should be careful until I get on birth control."

"Negative," I say, shaking my head. "Damage is done. My boys are on the ground running."

"Did you just talk about your sperm in military form?" she asks, laughing.

"I mean, I'm not going to toot my horn, but my boys are probably already trying to infiltrate," I say, leaning back and stretching.

"We just got back together," she says softly, and I get up now and walk over to her. I rip the elastic out of her hair and pick her up, her legs wrapping around my waist automatically.

"If I didn't leave," I start, walking over and sitting on the couch, and she straddles me. "Would we not be trying?"

"Probably," she answers honestly, and her hands now lay on my chest. Lifting herself just a bit, she reaches down and pulls my cock out of my boxers. She slowly inches down on it until she's all the way down. "Missed you," she says, and I rip her shirt off and see love bites everywhere. My teeth marks are on both tits also. I hold her tits in my hands, squeezing her as she rides me.

She leans back just a bit, putting one hand on my knee while the other hand plays with her clit. It takes her a minute, but soon, she's panting. My thumbs pinch and roll her nipples, and, fuck, she could come just by me playing with her nipples. I watch her ride me, knowing she's getting closer and closer.

When she comes on my cock, I give her just a moment to recover before I'm picking her up and throwing her over the couch. Grabbing her by the hips, I fuck her hard. I pull her hair back, and she groans out, "Harder." She chants over and over again, and I see one hand playing with her clit the whole time and the other trying to hold herself up. "Right there."

"I'm there," I say, feeling my balls start to pull up. "I'm there." I slam into her one last time, and she comes again all over my cock, leaking down my balls. I empty myself into her again, throwing my head back. I slowly fuck her when I'm done coming in her, and then I slip out of her. "Time for a shower."

"Not together." She pushes me away. "You go first, and I'll go after."

"There is no fun in that." I pick her up and throw her over my shoulder, slapping her ass. "Don't do that." I try not to laugh, knowing that it excites her, and she may say no more, but five minutes in the shower, and I know she'll want me again just as much as I want her.

Sitting on the bed, I'm waiting for her to get ready when she sticks her head out of the closet. "Where are we going again?" she asks, coming out of the closet wearing a gray and white summer dress with spaghetti straps. The dress flows around her calves, and she slips on flip-flops. I'm wearing shorts and a white button-down top with my own flip-flops. She comes to me, and I open my legs as she stands in the middle of them. "You look so handsome." She leans down and kisses my lips.

"If we don't go," I say, getting up and grabbing her by the hand, "we will never leave."

"If it was up to you," she tells me, "I'd be naked and chained to the bed."

"Don't pretend that you wouldn't like that." I wink at her, and she just blushes. We get into the truck to head over to my grandparents' house and pull up. "I think we should be good," I say, and she smiles at me.

"They would never say no to you," she tells me, getting out of the truck and walking with me. Her hand is in mine like it's supposed to be, and I bring our hands to my mouth and kiss her fingers.

"Everyone is going to know we're together," I say as we get closer to the backyard, and I hear more voices today than any other time.

"It shows you've been away from home for a long time," she tells me, looking over at me. "The news we were together spread yesterday when you made out with me half the day." She laughs. "Have you looked around?" she asks, and I finally look around. "Half the town showed up today to see if we'd appear."

"You think so?" I ask, and when we walk around the corner to the backyard, there is no denying that they are here for this.

"See all the prying eyes." She leans closer to me, and I stop her from walking and turn her around to face me.

"Well, if they are already talking, we might as well give them something to talk about," I say, grabbing her face and kissing her lips. "You know, just in case they were confused."

She shakes her head and just lets me kiss her. We spend the rest of the afternoon getting warm wishes from everyone.

"It's about time you got your head out of your behind," my grandmother says to me when I go to say hello to her. She grabs my face, just as she used to do when I was younger.

Kallie is the next one to grab us, her smile all over her face as she blinks away tears.

"I knew it would always end up like this," she says and then looks over at my father, who just stands away. "Jacob, didn't I tell you?"

He swallows, and the sadness in his eyes hits me in the stomach. I was shot and left for dead. I was beaten to within an inch of my life, and I've never felt more helpless than I do at this moment right here. "Great news." He nods, never making eye contact with me, and he turns to walk away. Kallie blinks tears away, smiling at us, and walks away, slipping her arm with his.

"You need to talk to him." I hear from beside me, and I smile at Emily, knowing that I have no choice. It needs to be done. "The longer you go, the worse it will be." I don't say anything to her, the lump forming in my throat.

My mother comes to us next. "Does this mean I can finally give Emily back her money?" She winks at Emily, who shakes her head.

"That house is mine," she says, slipping her arms around my waist. The rest of the day slips by, and when we get into the truck, she looks over at me. "Do you want to swing by the house and get the rest of your clothes?" she asks as she fastens her seat belt.

I smirk, turning to her. "Is this your way of asking me to move in?"

She shakes her head and turns to look at me, putting her back against the door. "Is that your way of telling me that I can kick you out?"

"I live there," I say. "I've been living there since Tuesday." Her mouth opens. "I gave Casey back the key on Wednesday."

"But you just brought over one bag." She picks up her hand, showing me one finger.

"That's all my stuff," I say. "Never had more than a couple

of shirts and pairs of jeans. I wasn't into material things. Besides, the only thing I had that was of great value to me was your picture, and I carried that with me everywhere," I say. She gets quiet and looks out the window, and when I pull up to the house and turn off the car, she rips her seat belt off and crawls in my lap, grabbing my face in her hands.

"I want to buy you stuff," she says with tears running down her face. "I want to buy you sweaters and shirts, an iPad, a laptop, all of it. I'm going to buy it, and we are going to put it in our house."

"Baby," I say softly. "I don't need any of that; I just need you. Besides, my most cherished item is right here." I rub my nose against her. "Your heart."

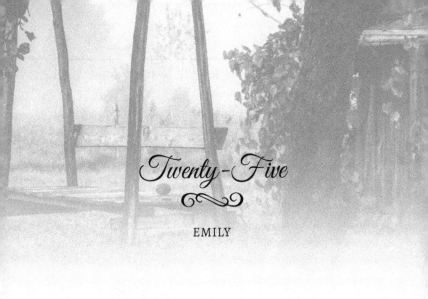

Twenty-Five

EMILY

"Wake up." I hear his voice softly, and I want to push him away. "It's almost time."

"For what?" I grumble and cuddle deeper in the bed.

"It's almost sunrise. Come on, get up so we can go watch it." He slips his hand around my naked waist. It's been three days since we've been officially back together, three days of waking up with him, three days of cooking for him, three days of him making love to me every single chance he got, even when he came home at lunchtime because he forgot something. Three days of bliss, three days, and it's like he never left me. "You can sleep when I leave," he tells me even though he knows I won't go to bed after he leaves, especially since I have to go clean out my classroom today.

"We can miss today," I grumble, and the covers are thrown off us, and the cold air hits my body right away. "Ethan, it's cold," I say, covering my nipples that are starting to pebble, and he moans as his hand reaches out to roll one of them. "Go away and watch the sunrise."

"It's better with you there." He leans down, taking a nipple in his mouth. "Just put the robe on," he says, and I know what that means. He wants easy access to me, and of course, I'm going to give it to him.

"Fine," I say, huffing out of bed. "But you're doing all the work." I look over and see his eyes go big. "What?"

"I didn't think I hit you that hard," he says, and I turn to see that his handprint is on my ass, and I laugh.

"You didn't. At least, I don't think you did." I grab my robe. "If something happens to me and they have to cut off my clothes, I don't know what they are going to think." I look down. "I have hickeys on both breasts, two on my stomach, and on my thigh. And let's not forget your teeth marks everywhere." I shake my head.

"Why do they need to see you naked?" he says, getting up. His cock is already at half mast, but it's always at half mast.

"You never know. I could get into an accident," I say, putting on the robe and tossing him his shorts. "It's still dark outside."

"I know," he says, slipping on his shorts. "You know I like to slide into you when the sun rises."

I shake my head. "You like to slide into me no matter what time it is." He laughs, holding my hand and pulling me outside. I look down, but when we step outside, the soft yellow lights make me look up. I stop walking when I see that the backyard has been transformed.

There are tea lights hanging from every tree branch and lanterns form a path to the middle of the yard. "What's going on?" I ask, looking around at how magical it looks in the moonlight. "What's all this?"

"This," he says, looking at me, "is part of your fifth birthday gift." He kisses me, bringing me to the middle of the yard. The lights hanging from the trees above my head light up everything.

"This is so beautiful," I say, smiling. "When did you do all this?"

"As soon as you fell asleep, I got to work. I mean, I had some help. Quinn and Keith started before I came out."

I gasp. "We had sex in the kitchen." I hold the robe closed at my chest. "And then the counter."

"I closed the shades," he tells me.

"But," I start to stutter. "We aren't exactly quiet."

"No." He taps my nose. "You aren't quiet."

I put my hands on my face. "What if they heard us?" I close my eyes now and put my hands to my stomach. "Oh my god, oh my god, oh my god. I teach Keith."

"They didn't hear anything," he tries to tell me. "Trust me, if they did, they would have told me about it."

"I don't know if that makes it better or worse," I say and see that he is looking at me strangely.

"Sunrise," he says my name, and then I smile at the softness of his voice. "I don't even know what to say," he starts, and my heart beats faster.

"Oh my god," I say, putting my hand to my mouth. "You're leaving."

He looks at me, not saying anything. "I can't believe this is happening." I put my hand to my mouth. "Oh my god." The tears come automatically. "How could you do this?"

"I'm not going anywhere," he says, holding my face in his hands. "Baby, I am not going anywhere." He kisses my lips. "It's the opposite of that."

"What does that mean?" I ask, not sure what he is trying to say.

"It means ..." he says, getting down on one knee in front of me. My hands fly to my mouth this time. "It means that I'm here to stay. When I woke up in that hospital bed five months ago, my mind was all over the place. They tried to fill in the blanks," he says. "Tried telling me about the mission that went wrong, but I didn't hear it. I didn't see it. I had nightmares for months. I spent night after night piecing everything together.

The doctor told me that it was my brain's way of protecting certain things. Then one night, it just all came crashing back. I had spent the day sitting by the lake near the house, dissecting every single dream. That night when I went to bed, it was as if I was transported back." The tears run down both our faces. "The guy was beating the shit out of me. Kicking my ribs, and then he took his gun out and shot me. The sound echoed so loud in the room, all I heard was loud buzzing, and then they came in and rescued me."

"Oh my god." I put my hands on his face and sob while I kiss his lips.

"I kept calling for you," he tells me, breaking my heart that I wasn't able to be there with him. "I whispered your name over and over again. All I wanted was to see you one more time before I left this earth. I just wanted one more chance to tell you how much I loved you. I wanted one more chance to tell you that you made my life magical. I wanted one more chance to marry you and be the father of our children. I wanted one more sunrise." He smiles through his own tears.

"Sunrise, I want to watch every single sunrise with you. I want to hold your hand while we sit side by side. I want to fight with you just so we can make up. I want to be the one who dries your tears and makes you smile. I know I asked you this before, and I know that I don't deserve another chance, but it's always been you." He reaches into the pocket of his shorts and takes out the brown box he held just five years ago. "I gave you back everything that was yours last time except this." He opens it, and there is the ring. "Emily, will you marry me?" he asks. "Will you make my nightmares become sweet dreams?"

I nod my head as my body shakes with sobs. "Yes." He slips the ring on my finger and gets up, pulling me to him and kissing me softly. "I'll marry you," I say, wiping the tears away from my cheeks.

He picks me up and turns us in a circle, celebrating. "I love you," I say, and he carries me toward the back door. "What are you doing? We have to celebrate in the hammock."

"No way in hell," he says, walking up the stairs. "I don't know if Quinn and Keith are out there." I throw my head back and laugh just as the sun rises.

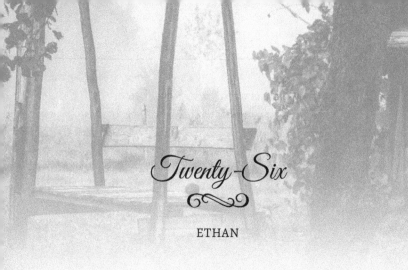

Twenty-Six

ETHAN

"Why are you so quiet?" she asks, and I look up at her. She leans against the counter, holding her cup of tea. She's wearing shorts and a shirt that goes off her shoulder with her hair piled on top of her head.

I look down at my plate and push around the food she just cooked. "I just." I look up at her and see the glistening of the ring on her hand. "I have to go and speak to my father."

"I think that's a good idea," she says softly, coming to me now and sitting down beside me. "It's time."

"I know it is," I say, my stomach turning. "I just, fuck ..." I put my head down. "I said some shitty fucking things."

"You did," she says, putting her hand on my neck. "And a coward would walk away, but you are going to go over there and make things right with him. You have to, Ethan. He's your dad."

I nod at her, knowing it's the truth, and when I kiss her goodbye ten minutes later, she shocks me by putting on her shoes. "Where are you going?"

"I'm not letting you go there all by yourself," she says.

Walking out of the house, she waits for me to walk out, holding up her hand to block the sun. "I mean, you have to talk to him by yourself, but I'm going to be there for you when it's over."

I don't even tell her that it's fine, and it'll be okay. Instead, I grab her hand and bring it to my lips. "I love you."

"You better," she says, and when we pull up to my father's house, my heart speeds up faster in my chest.

"Maybe we should have called before coming over," I say, tapping my finger on the steering wheel. "We'll come back," I say, but she is getting out of the truck, waiting for me. I take a huge deep breath and get out.

"It's going to be okay," she says, grabbing my hand as we walk up the walkway. I look around to see if anything has changed, and it all looks the same. "Should we ring the doorbell or just go in?" she asks, and I swear I feel like I'm going to be sick. She leans over and presses the bell, and we hear screaming from inside.

The door opens, and Kallie stands there with her hair piled on her head, and when she sees me, a big smile forms on her face. "Well, this is a wonderful surprise." She looks at us. "But why did you ring the doorbell?" She shakes her head. "Come on in."

Emily walks in first, and I follow her. Looking around, I see that the pictures on the wall are still the same. More have been added, but mine stopped when I turned twenty. The last picture they have of all the kids together was two months before I left. The smile on everyone's face is everything. "Hey, you guys." I hear Amelia and look over at her as she comes down the stairs. "I didn't know that you were coming over."

"It's a surprise," Kallie says, smiling. "Come in and stop acting like strangers." She looks at me. "This is your home."

I look down, unsure as to what to say. "Is Dad home?" I

ask, my voice low. Kallie looks over at me, and she has tears in her eyes.

"He's in the shed," she says. "They're all going fishing tomorrow, so he's making sure he has everything ready. Go out there."

I nod and look over at Emily, who just nods at me. "You'll be fine."

"He doesn't have his gun, does he?" I ask Kallie, and she just laughs. Yeah, he always has his gun on him. We were taught very young that if there was any danger, we had to run the other way while Dad ran toward the danger. I step out into the backyard and see the play structure he built for me when I was three. It looks like it hasn't been used in years. I don't have to walk far when he comes out of the shed, and when he sees me, he stops in his tracks. I'm suddenly back to when I was five years old, and all I wanted to do was hug my father.

"Hey," I say, lifting my hand. He just looks at me, almost as if he's scared to say anything to me. "I was wondering if we could talk," I start. As soon as the words are out of my mouth, I say, "I can come back. It's not that important."

"Why don't we go to the creek?" He motions with his head to the back of the yard, and I see the treehouse he built for me but then changed it into a real house for Amelia.

"It's seen better days," I say to him and walk down to the creek, both of us not saying anything. I swallow. "So how have you been?" I ask, making small talk, and it's the most awkward fucking conversation we've ever had.

"You came all this way to ask me how I've been?" He cuts to the chase before I do, and I just look at him. "How I've been?" He shakes his head.

"This is harder than I thought it would be," I say to him, and he looks down. "I'm sorry." He looks up. "I figure before I start saying anything, I should just start with that. I'm so sorry."

He laughs now bitterly. "You're sorry?" He looks up at the sky. "You're sorry."

"I know, Dad." When I say his name, his head snaps to mine.

"Oh, I'm your father now?" he asks, and he has tears in his eyes. "Now I'm your father. Five years ago, I was nothing to you," he says, his voice broken. "At least that is what you said to me." My eyes fill with tears as I see how much I've hurt him.

"I went to see him," I tell him, and he looks at me. "Liam." I don't say that he's my father because he isn't. "He came to the door and didn't even know who I was." I think back to that day, avoiding looking at my father while I tell him this part. "I told him who I was and," I exhale, "I don't know what I was expecting but he just looked at me like I was a pizza delivery person. He smiled at me, and stepped out of his house to make sure that no one heard our conversation. A conversation that lasted less than three minutes." I look at my father who just stands there looking at me waiting for me to finish before he says something. "He thanked me for coming," I laugh bitterly, "and wished me well right after he told me that I wasn't really welcomed." The hurt now coming back. "When I left here, I was broken," I say. "I drove away, and I was numb. I didn't know what to believe or what to think." I walk over to the rock and sit down on it. "I was so fucking lost, Dad. I just ..." I put my head down. "I did stupid things," I say. "Took risks with my life for nothing just because I thought I didn't care if I lived or died. I went on missions that I shouldn't have been on, but I did it because there was nothing to come back to, so it didn't matter if I died."

"If you died?" he says. "If you died." He puts his hands to his chest. "Do you know what that would do to me? I had to bury one son. Do you think I wanted to bury another one? I was numb when you left. I would call your phone number every single hour even though I had the phone in my hand and knew you wouldn't answer. I would call and leave you messages. I would call just to hear your voice." The tears come down his face. "I wanted just a minute with you to tell you that I loved you." I try to say something, but it's his turn to let it all out, and I have to give it to him. I have to hear the pain he suffered. I need to accept I did that to him. "Casey found you and came to see me. I got on a plane to come to you, but then they stopped me at the gate." My mouth opens. "Said they didn't have anyone there with your name." It's then that I see everything unravel. What I did to him was so fucked up I didn't deserve his love. I didn't deserve anything he gave me. "I waited outside those gates for two days, and then I left. I came back here, and I would wait. I waited for Casey to give me a crumble of news. Waited every single day, not knowing if you were alive or dead. Not knowing if you needed me, not knowing if you were okay. I couldn't help you." He throws up his hand. "Useless, that is what I was."

"You came to see me?" I ask, still shocked at that. "I didn't know."

"I have to think that there was a reason for that. Some sick and twisted reason that God kept you away from me." The anguish pours out of him. "That rock." He points at the rock I'm sitting on. "I would come out here every single night after dinner when the kids would get ready for bed, and I would talk to you. I would hope you were okay. I would replay every single fucking memory I had of you over and over—year after year. From the first time they placed you in my arms, I was so fucking scared. I was never more scared of anything in my life. But you stopped crying as if you knew that I was going to make everything okay for you. From the first time you fell asleep on my chest to the time you came to me and told me you were getting married, I was so proud of the man you were. So fucking proud. I didn't care whose DNA you had. You were mine. You are mine." He points at his chest.

"I am, Dad," I say finally. "I was a little shit, and I was brought up better than that," I say. "You taught me better than that."

"I did," he tells me.

"I died," I say, and he gasps. "Five months ago, I was held as a prisoner when our mission went haywire."

"Oh my god." He puts his hands in front of his mouth.

"They beat me," I tell him. "Tortured me, and at one point, I begged God to take me. But ..." I wipe my eyes. "You know people say that you see the bright white light, and I always thought it was a lie until I saw it myself. I knew at that moment I was dead, knew it in my heart. And then all this sadness came over me. I was going to die, and my family wouldn't know. I wanted one more chance to tell you that you were the best dad anyone could ever have. I wanted to tell you that I want to be just like you. I wanted to hug you, and I wanted you to kiss me right behind the ear, just like you always did. Even when I was twenty." I turn my head now. "It's why I put my cross tattoo there."

"Son," he says, coming to me and hugging me, and I cry in his arms, just like I did when I was younger. "I'm so sorry I wasn't there." This right here, this is who my father is, this man who I hurt with all my words holds me as he has always done my whole life. Holding me up when I can't stand, he makes sure that I get my strength from him.

"I'm so sorry, Dad." I hug him harder than I ever have in my whole life. I hug him, clinging to him. "I'm so sorry."

"It's okay, son," he says, and then he lets go of me. "You always hurt the ones you love first. You know why?" he asks. "It's because the ones you love will forgive you."

"I don't know if I deserve your forgiveness," I say honestly. "But I'm going to prove to you that I'm sorry."

"This," he says, squeezing my shoulder. "Coming here,

being here, shows me how sorry you are." He wipes his tears. "Are you staying?"

"I asked Emily to marry me this morning," I say. "I want to marry her here. I want to build a family here."

"Then there is only one more thing to say." He smiles at me. "Welcome home, son!"

Twenty-Seven

EMILY

"Are you okay?" I ask when he walks back into the house with Jacob beside him. Both of them look like they went through the war zone.

"I am," he says, smiling, and I see his eyes are red from crying. "It's going to be okay." He wraps his arms around the top of my chest, and then Jacob goes over to Kallie and kisses her neck.

"Do you want to go fishing tomorrow?" Jacob looks over at Ethan, who just looks at me, and I try to hide the smile that is filling my face.

"Yeah," Ethan says. "I'd like that a lot."

"Well, get ready because we leave at seven," Jacob says to Ethan, and we spend the rest of the day with Kallie and Jacob, and when we leave, neither of us says anything. When we walk into the house, he takes me in his arms.

"Are you happy?" I ask when he buries his face in my neck while we lie in the hammock, watching the stars.

"I am," he says. "It was rough with my dad." He starts to say, "He gave up everything to love me, and I threw it away as if it was nothing. When, in reality, it was everything."

"It was," I say, and that night when he makes love to me, it's slow, and he holds me all night long. When the sun rises the next day, we are sitting on the back stoop while he waits for Jacob to pick him up.

"Have fun," I say, kissing him goodbye and then waving to him. I slip back into bed, but I toss and turn and finally give up.

I'm making myself some tea when there is a knock on the door. Walking down the hallway to the front door, I see Savannah standing there, looking out. "Hey," I say to her, and she turns around and smiles at me.

"Sorry for dropping by." She turns and wipes a tear away. "I didn't think coming here would make me cry."

I smile at her. "You don't ever have to be sorry about stopping by. Come in." I move aside, and she walks into the house. "This is a nice surprise. I was going to call Jenna to come over and have tea with me, but this might be better." She smiles at me, and we walk down the hallway. "Would you like some cold tea or coffee?"

"Um, do you have whiskey?" she asks, and my eyes get big. "I need the encouragement."

"Why does that scare me?" I ask. Walking over, I grab the whiskey and a glass, bringing it to her.

She takes the top off and pours herself a shot and then looks at me, wincing, "Horrible."

"Not for the faint of heart, I'm told." I stand here in front of her.

She leans over and grabs her purse, taking out a paper. "Before you say anything, hear me out." She looks down, tapping the paper in front of her that is folded out. "I got pregnant by accident of course," she tells me, and I just look at her as she pours another shot, and this time, the wince is less. "Smoother the second time." She laughs, wiping her mouth. "Ethan's father is an asshole. I should have seen it then, but I was too swept up in being loved by someone to even notice I was being played."

"I'm so sorry," I say, wanting to reach out and hold her.

"After I found out I was pregnant, I was beside myself. I was eighteen, living alone, my mother, at her best day, was barely around. I had no one, and Liam didn't want anything to do with me, so I went to his father, and, well, that was even worse." She takes another shot. "He threw two hundred dollars at me and told me to take out the trash." She wipes the tears from her eyes, and I can't help the tears that fall out of my eyes. "I was always known as that kid. The one who was not good enough for anyone or anything. No matter how successful I was in school, no one let me forget I was trash."

"That's so wrong," I say, not even imagining how it was.

"So I played a game with the devil," she says, looking down. "I went to his office and blackmailed him." She takes another shot. "Fuck, this is harder than I thought."

"You don't have to do this," I say.

"I want to," she tells me. "I blackmailed him, and with that money, I bought my bar and this house." She smiles now. "For once, I had a home. A real home. Not just for me but also for Ethan. I was determined for him to have a home. For him to know that he was loved, for him to know that he had a home where he was always going to be safe." She looks around. "This is his," she tells me. "It was always supposed to be his. Let me give this to you guys."

"But I bought it from you," I say, and she smiles and looks down. "What did you do?"

"I never signed the papers," she says, and I open my mouth. "I'm sorry. I'm so sorry, but," she hands me the papers, "your money is all in this account."

I grab the paper and open it. "You took payments monthly," I say, looking to see the savings account that was open. "I paid the taxes."

"You did," she tells me. "And that is for the kids." She gives me another paper. "When you have them."

"I don't believe this," I say, shocked. "You knew I wanted this house."

"I knew that if he came back that he was going to get you back. I knew that, in the end, this would be his."

"But what if I'd married Drew?" I ask, and she shakes her head.

"There was no way that was ever going to happen. Worst case ..." She smirks. "And I'm saying worst case, I was going to drag Ethan back."

"I can't believe this." I look down at the paper. "I ..."

"Let me give this to you guys," she tells me.

"I know where he gets it from now," I say, shaking my head. "You know he's not going to want this, right?"

"He isn't going to argue with me." She shrugs. "And if he does, I'll play my ace card."

"I'm afraid to ask," I say, and she smirks. "I also don't want to know."

"It's better if you don't," she says. The door opens, and I hear Ethan calling my name.

I look over and see that it's earlier than I thought he would be home. "Sunrise, I'm back."

"Your mom is here," I say in case he says something no one wants their mother to hear.

"Oh, hey, Mom," he says, walking to her and kissing her cheek. "This is nice." He walks around and comes down to kiss me, seeing my eyes red. "What happened?"

"Nothing," I say, kissing his lips and hugging his waist. "Your mom came over to give you something."

"Did she?" He looks at his mother.

"This is yours," she says, handing him a white paper, and he lets me go to open it, and I read it with him, the house in his name, and he looks at the paper and then at me.

"This is your house," he says. "You bought it."

I shrug my shoulder. "I thought I did, but it turns out, I was wrong."

"But," he says. "But it's yours." He looks at his mother. "It's her house."

"That's up to you to decide," she tells him.

"I'm not taking this." He hands her back the paper. "I don't want it. If you want, we will buy it from you."

"Negative," she says, leaning back in the chair. "You left us for five years, and all I could do was hope that you would come back. Now you're here, and this is what needs to happen. This house was always yours from the moment I bought it. I've never asked you for anything in five years," she says, and now I know the ace up her sleeve.

"Oh, god," Ethan says. "You get to use that excuse one time," he tells her. "But I'll only accept it if you add Emily's name to it."

"You don't have to do it," I say. "I bought this house for you anyway."

"I'll add Emily's name," Savannah says. "Now, I have to go and get ready for a mayor dinner, which I hate." She gets up and comes over to hug Ethan. "You stink."

"Of what?" he says.

"Fish guts, sunscreen, worms, and horse." She scrunches up her nose. "Now, I want you guys over for dinner tomorrow."

"No can do," Ethan says. "I have to go close up the cabin. I sold it."

"What?" I look at him. "You ..."

"No use having it," he says as if it's nothing, "so I sold it to one of the boys I knew. I thought we could go up there for a week or so." I don't have time to answer him.

"Well, you better call me when you guys get back,"

Savannah says, giving me a hug. "And text me when you get there."

"Ready to take a shower?" he asks, picking me up, and my legs wrap around him automatically.

"I don't want to wet my hair," I tell him. "I just washed it."

"Sunrise," he says my name. "You know that I love washing your hair."

"No," I say over my shoulder as I turn on the water. "You love holding my hair while fucking me."

"I do love doing that." He smiles wide, taking off his shirt and tossing it into the basket. "Now get your ass in there and sit down. I didn't eat my breakfast this morning." He slaps my ass, and the way he says the words makes my knees weak, so I do the only thing I can do. I walk into the shower and sit my ass down while he buries his face between my legs.

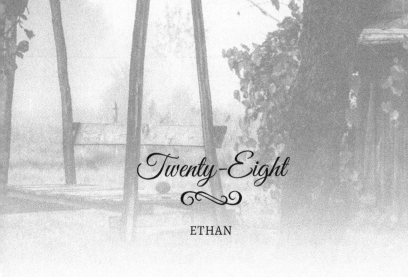

Twenty-Eight

ETHAN

"I'm going to miss this view," Emily says from on top of me after we finished watching the sunrise sitting on the porch of the cabin, her naked back to my chest. A cover wrapped around us, and my cock buried still inside her have become a morning ritual up here. We got here six days ago. I was nervous to show her the little cabin, afraid she would run for the hills. But instead, she smiled big and asked two things —if there was a toilet and hot water. We spent every day hiking and the nights with the lights on, getting lost in each other.

"I'm going to miss being naked with you outside and not caring if anyone can see you," I say, holding her tits in my hands and rolling her nipples between my fingers, and she winces. "Does that hurt?"

"They are just sensitive," she says, looking at me sideways. "That is all." She smiles and moves her hips, making my cock wake up now. "Is he ready for round two?"

"You mean four," I say. "You forget the twice before we came outside."

"We got it in six times yesterday," she says, and my hands

hold both tits as she rides me again, and her moans start and echo in the forest. "Also, never fucking against a tree."

"It was one splinter." I bite her shoulder, and the cover falls off her, and I see she is playing with herself.

"It was a splinter in my ass." Her hips go around and then she gets up and slides down again faster and faster.

"You didn't want to put your hands on the ground, so how else was I going to get inside you?" I roll her nipples, and she winces again, so I move my hands to her hips, and I help her move up and down. When she yells out that she's coming, it takes a minute more for me to follow her. She gets up off me now or else before we both know it we'll go for round two.

"What time is he coming to get the keys?" she asks, looking at me naked standing there with the sun behind her. "Stop looking at me like that. I have shit to do like shower and wash the sheets."

"You don't have to wash the sheets." I get up, grabbing the cover, and walk into the cabin with her. "He's a soldier. We sleep on dusty cots half the time."

"We've had sex in that bed. It smells of sex," she says, shaking her head and walking over to strip the bed.

"You know what I'm going to miss," I say, and she looks up, holding the sheets in her arms. "You being naked all the time."

She throws her head back and laughs. "I wouldn't be naked all the time if you gave me my clothes back." Another thing I've done is take her clothes and hide them. Knowing no one can see her and having her naked around me is so much better than her in my shirt.

"I gave you clothes to wear out on our hike," I remind her. "But I've also decided that every Saturday will be naked Saturday in the house."

"In our house?" she asks. "The house in the city? Where people just drop by, and we have all those windows."

"I'll tell them they can't come over on Saturday," I say, and she gasps.

"You are not going to tell anyone that they can't come over because it's naked Saturday." She walks out and tosses the sheets in the wash. I make her tea, and by the time the guy comes to get the keys, we are already packed up and ready to head back home. "Do you want a minute to say goodbye?"

"Nah," I say, looking at the house. "This was never home."

I open the door for her and toss Carey my keys. "Hope you find what you are looking for," I say, and he looks at me. His brown eyes are almost like mine were five years ago —empty.

"I'm looking to disappear," he says, running his hands through his short black hair, and I nod at him. "Figured this was the perfect place."

"It is," I say. "Let me know if you need anything." He just looks at me. "Even if it's just to talk."

"Thanks," he says and turning around, walking to the house, he grabs a small duffel bag and throws it over his shoulder. I get in the truck and see that Emily is wiping a tear from her eye.

"What's wrong?" I ask, and she shakes her head.

"That little boy is so lost," she says. "You can see the anguish in his eyes. Do you know his story?" she asks, and I shake my head. I don't fill her in on the talk from the other soldiers either. It's his story to tell, not mine.

The drive home is spent with her dozing off. "I'm so tired," she says when we pull up to our house. "All that fresh air has me ready to fall."

"Go to bed, and I'll get the things out of the truck." I kiss her, and she just nods, and when I finish unloading the truck, I find her curled up in a ball. I slip into bed beside her, and even though I find her naked, she doesn't budge. She sleeps through the night and is dragging ass the whole day after.

When I come in, I find her sleeping on the couch, and I call my mother.

"Mom," I say as soon as she answers the phone. "I don't know what to do."

"What happened?" she asks, and I hear a door close, and the noise around her is now quiet.

"Emily keeps sleeping," I say, and it suddenly sounds so stupid even to me. "She gets up to eat and then goes back to bed."

"Is she sick?" she asks. "Does she have a fever?" I walk to the couch and feel her head.

"No, she's fine," I say, and she opens her eyes, looking at me, confused. "She's up now."

"What are you doing?" she says, moving away from my hand.

"Mom, she has no fever," I tell my mother and see Emily close her eyes again.

"I'm taking her to the emergency room," I tell my mother and Emily, who opens her eyes again.

"I'll meet you there," my mother says at the same time Emily says, "No, I'm fine."

"Honey," my mother says. "Go talk to Emily and let me know what you decide. If you want, I'll come with you guys."

"Okay, Mom," I say, hanging up the phone and getting on my knees, but Emily sits up now. "Seriously, maybe you caught something at the cabin."

"I didn't catch anything at the cabin," she tells me, pushing me away, getting up, and then walking to the bedroom with me following her. "I was," she starts to tell me, and she has this stick in her hand. "I had this whole thing I was going to say, but I'm just too tired."

"What do you mean?" I say, grabbing the stick and seeing what it is.

Pregnant

Is written in the middle of the small clear window. "Oh my god," I say, putting my hand to my mouth.

"I know it's crazy." She shakes her head. "Jenna brought it over today, and well, I didn't think anything of it, but I am late by two days."

"You're having my baby?" I say, my chest feeling so full it might crack open. "Holy shit. My boys got the job done." She looks at me shocked now. "What? We had sex six times a day. How did you not think you were going to end up pregnant?"

"You wanted me pregnant?" she asks, and I shrug but then smile.

"Do you not want to be pregnant by me?" I ask, suddenly getting scared that she doesn't want this.

"Of course I do, but I didn't expect to get knocked up month one," she tells me and then puts her hand on her stomach. "We've made a baby."

"We did," I say, smiling.

"Baby McIntyre," she says, and I look at her.

I walk to her and kiss her lips. "I have to do something," I say. "One last thing. I was going to do this at a later date, but I need to do it now."

"Are you going to tell me what it is?" she asks and I nod.

"As soon as I get back." I kiss her lips. "Lie down and don't move."

"What?" she says to me.

"You have to rest, and you need to get medical leave. I'm going to see about maybe getting a wheelchair and stuff so you don't have to stand. Or I can just ask Grandma to move in here and help out until the baby is born," I say, grabbing my keys, and she just looks at me. "I'll be back."

"Can you bring back normal Ethan when you do that?" she tells me, and I run back in and kiss her.

I get in the truck and rush over to my father's house. I'm about to ring the doorbell when it opens, and Travis comes out, and he smells like he's in heat. "What the fuck is that smell?"

"It's Abercrombie," he says, puffing out his chest. "It's what the guys wear."

"To attract bugs maybe. Jesus," I say, fanning the air away from my nose. "Is Dad here?"

"Yeah, he's inside with Mom. They were making out." He grimaces. "So gross."

I walk inside, and sure enough, he has her in his arms, and he's talking in her ear. "Hey," I say, and Kallie looks up and smiles at me. "I ..." I say, pointing at the hall. "Travis let me in."

"Stop that shit," Kallie says. "And the next time you use the bell, I'm going to Taser you."

"Isn't that illegal?" I ask, my eyebrows shooting up.

"I know someone," she says, and my father laughs at her.

"What's up? You look frazzled." He looks at me and grabs the beer that's on the counter and brings it to his lips.

"Can I speak with you?" I ask and then look at Kallie. "Kind of man things."

"Oh, good God." She puts her hands up. "I don't even want to know. The last time you said that, you put condoms on all my bananas."

"I was practicing," I say as she walks away. "I got an A in that class."

"Yet, you failed biology!" she shouts back.

"That was gross. They wanted me to cut open a frog, Kallie. You know I don't like those things!" I shout at her retreating back and look at my father, who tries not to laugh. "I hate frogs."

"I know, trust me, I know," he says. "So what's up?"

"Emily is pregnant." I come right out and say it, and I swear I can't help but smile so big I think my face is going to crack. "She's having my baby."

"Holy shit," my father says and comes over to me and hugs me, slapping my back. "My boy is going to be a father," he says, wiping his own tear away. "I knew this day would come." He slaps my chest. "My boy, a father." He puts his hand in front of his mouth. "God, I hope you have a girl. She's going to be so beautiful, and you are going to hate it. You know, with boys, you have to worry about one penis; with girls, it's all the other penises you have to worry about. Especially with Emily's looks, you're fucked."

"Nah," I tell him. "It's a boy. I feel it in my bones."

"I felt you were a boy, too," he says. "We used to fight over finding out, and your mother never wanted to know. She wanted it to be a surprise, but I felt it."

"I want your name," I tell him. My heart speeds up, my palms get all fucking sweaty, and I feel sick in the pit of my stomach. "I want my kids to have your name. I want them to be McIntyres. I know that changing it was a slap in the face, and there is nothing I can say that will justify that. I know I need to earn that name," I tell him. "I know this, and I promise you that I'll earn your name back," I say, wiping my tears. "But I can't have my kids have any other name than McIntyre. I want them to be McIntyres."

"Son," he says softly. "I don't give a shit what is written on any fucking paper." He walks to me. "In here." He points at my heart. "It's McIntyre." I nod, and he takes me in his arms.

"Thank you," I say, "for not making this harder than it should be."

"You'll be a dad before you know it, and then you'll get it," he says, squeezing my shoulder. "You want them safe, you want them healthy, and you want them happy. The rest is just icing on the cake."

"I have to get back to Emily. I just left her there," I say, and he rolls his lips. "I needed to make sure this was okay before anything. She's going to have my name, too."

"I can't wait," he tells me. "I'd be honored."

"I told her she isn't allowed to move, and she looked like she was going to stab me," I tell my father, and this time, he laughs. "I also mentioned that she shouldn't go back to work and that Grandma can move in."

"What?" he asks, shocked. "Why?"

"She shouldn't move for the baby," I say, and he shakes his head.

"Son," he whispers, "marry her before she changes her mind."

Epilogue One

EMILY

"Is she sitting down?" I hear Ethan through the door and look over at Savannah.

"You're lucky that I love your son with everything I have," I say to her "or I would leave until after the baby is born."

"Would you relax?" I hear Jenna tell him in the hallway. "How do you want her to walk down the aisle? Do you think she is going to float down there?"

"I can carry her," he says, and I groan.

"I will take care of this." Savannah gets up and comes over to me. "Just remember it's going to be so much worse when he sees you in labor." She hugs me and walks out in her mother of the groom dress.

"I would never expect him to be like this," Kallie says from beside me.

"He followed me into the bathroom the other day," I say, "because I said I had cramps."

She rolls her lips. "I had gas."

"Oh, honey," she says, trying not to laugh, and I glare at her at the same time our child kicks. My hand goes down to my belly, and I look in the mirror.

The lace dress fits me like a glove, hugging my every curve and showing off my little baby bump. The little lace cap sleeves and then the light pink belt right on top of my bump, going tight to the knee and then kicking off into a mermaid style with a little train. "This is so not how I thought I would look when I got married," I tell everyone in the room. "I look …"

"You look beautiful," Kallie says, and the door opens, and Savannah comes back in.

"Okay, so if we don't get you down the aisle, I think he's just breaking down the door," she says, and I shake my head. When we found out five months ago that we were pregnant, he went from laid-back to over the top. He refused to have sex with me, thinking he was shaking the water in the sac and making our child do the wave. Only when the doctor told him it was okay did he give in, not counting the times I would sneak up on him when he was sleeping.

"Let's get this over with," I say, grabbing the flowers and then walking to the door.

"That's so romantic," Chelsea says. "What everyone always wants to hear. Let's get this thing over with." All I do is glare at her, and she looks at me. "I can't wait to have normal Emily back."

I laugh now, and when I stand outside the closed door, I hear the pianist start to play, and then the door opens, and I look down the aisle at him wearing a suit with his hands in front of him, and his face breaks out into a smile. I start walking down the aisle, and all I can do is look at him. When I finally make it down the aisle, he grabs my hand and brings it to his mouth. "You look amazing," he says, "but you could have tripped."

"Shut up," I say. "Don't ruin this for me or so help me God …" Leaning into him, I say, "I'll say no."

I glare at him, and he just laughs at me, grabbing my face

in his hands. "You wouldn't dare, Sunrise," he says, kissing my lips.

"Well, it seems that we have gotten a little bit off of the path," the preacher says, making everyone laugh. I hand my bouquet to Jenna, who just smiles at me through her tears.

"Now, shall we start at the beginning?"

"Yes," Ethan says, and he holds my hand the whole time. I don't even hear all the things he says because I'm too busy looking over at Ethan. He is still the handsome boy I fell in love with under the stars—the boy who waited until I was fifteen before he kissed me.

"I've been told that Ethan and Emily will say their own vows," the preacher says, and he tells us to face each other and hold hands. "Emily." I smile at him and then look at Ethan.

"Ethan," I say, suddenly nervous. "My Ethan." I look into his blue eyes, and all I can do is feel loved. "I knew I loved you when I was fifteen years old, and I snuck out of my house to watch the sunrise with you. I knew lying there looking up at the stars that I wanted you to be with me forever. When we would see stars flying through the sky, and you would tell me to make a wish, it would always be the same thing. To always be with you." A tear comes out of my eye, and he lets my hand go to wipe it away with his thumb. "Thank you for loving me with everything you are. Thank you for loving our child to the point of driving me insane. Thank you for being you, thank you for choosing me to walk beside you for the rest of our lives. Thank you for giving me the best life anyone could ask for." I smile at him, and he leans forward and kisses me softly.

"Sorry," he tells the preacher. "I don't like it when she cries."

"You are forgiven," the preacher says. "Now it's your turn."

"Emily," he says, "Sunrise ..." I look down and then up

again. "I don't know where to start, so I'm going to start at the beginning. Asking you to be my girlfriend was the best thing I ever did." I can't help but smile. "Falling in love with you came so easy. I didn't even know it was happening until one day I looked over at you and my heart skipped a beat, and I knew I could never be without you. My body, my mind, my soul, and my heart. They are all yours. Everything." He sheds a tear, and it's my turn to wipe it away. "Everything that I am is because I want to be that better person for you. I am going to hold your hand every single morning when we watch the sunrise. I'm going to wipe away your tears when you cry. I'm going to hold you up when you fall. I am going to hold you in my arms every single night while we sleep. I belong to you, my heart belongs to you in this life, in our past life, and in our next life, it will always be you." He comes to me and kisses me and then looks over at the preacher. "She's my wife now."

"Not yet," he tells him. "You have to exchange rings. Emily, place the ring on Ethan's finger and repeat after me."

He says the words, and I repeat after him. "I give you this ring as a token of my love, and I promise that from this day forward, I will love you, honor you, and cherish you, in sickness and in health for all of the days of our lives." I slide the ring down his finger, and he smiles big, then he takes my hand and repeats after the preacher.

"Emily, I give you this ring as a token of my love, and I promise you that I will love you, honor you, cherish you all of the days of our lives, in sickness and in health." He slides the ring down and then kisses them.

"Ethan," he says. "You may now kiss your bride."

"Finally," he says, making everyone laugh. He grabs my face like he always does and brings me in closer. "Forever, Sunrise," he says, kissing me on the lips. Our friends and family cheer and clap while he kisses me and then gets down and kisses my stomach, rubbing his hands over it like he does every single day.

The preacher now announces, "Ladies and gentlemen, I give you Mr. and Mrs. Ethan McIntyre."

Epilogue Two

ETHAN

Four Months Later

"You are doing so well," I say, pushing back the hair on her head as she tries to push again. The agony is all over her face, and it's taking everything in my power not to punch the wall.

"It hurts," she tells me, her voice going so low. "I'm so tired." She looks at me, and her face is pale because she's been in labor for two days now. Her water finally broke fourteen hours ago. We came when she started getting contractions, but we were sent home, and until they were four minutes apart, we were told that it was just the course it would take.

"I know you are, Sunrise," I say. "And if I could, I would take away all your pain."

"Okay, Emily," the doctor says from between her legs. "It's time to push again."

"I can't," Emily says, crying. "I can't."

"You can," I say, holding her hand. "Look at me," I say. "Look at me." She turns her head. "You are the strongest person I know. You can do this."

"Push," the doctor says, and Emily grips my hand as hard as she can and pushes while the doctor and the nurse both count to ten. "Again," the doctor says, and Emily grunts out when she finally gets to the next ten.

"I see a head," the nurse says from the other side of Emily. "Lots of hair."

"Okay, I need you to give us everything that you have," the doctor says, and Emily grips my hand again, and she does it. "One more push and your baby is going to be here," she says, and Emily pushes one more time, and then it happens so fast. The baby comes out, she suctions something out of the mouth, and the sound of crying fills the room. The doctor places the baby directly onto Emily's chest, and she sobs, holding the baby in her arms. My own tears pour down my face as I hug her and the baby in my arms. "It's a boy," the doctor says, and all I can hear is Emily sobbing as she talks to him.

"He's so beautiful," she says, kissing his head. "Ethan, look at our baby." She doesn't have to tell me because I can't take my eyes off him. He is perfect and pink and huge. The nurse smiles at us.

"Daddy," the doctor calls me. "Time to cut the cord." She hands me the scissors and tells me to cut between two yellow pegs.

"Okay, I have to get him cleaned up," the nurse says, taking the baby away from Emily, and I almost shout at her to bring him back.

"Ethan, go with him," she tells me, and I just shake my head.

"I'm not leaving you," I say, sitting next to her as the doctor finishes with her, my eye on the nurse in the corner as she does what she needs to do.

She comes back to us, our son wrapped in a blue blanket with a blue hat on his head. "He is a big boy at nine pounds, ten ounces." She places the baby in my arms, and I don't think I have ever felt a love like this. A love that is so unconditional that it just pours through your bones. Knowing that you are going to protect him, teach him, love him, it's a love that is so powerful nothing can break the bond. "Good job, Momma."

"Hey there," I tell him between tears, his eyes blinking open and closed as he takes in his new world. "I'm going to be by your side your whole life," I say, and he opens his mouth like he is going to answer me. "Sunrise," I say, and she looks at me. "What do we call him?"

She smiles. "Let's tell the family together."

I hand her the baby and walk out into the waiting room. I walk into the room, expecting for just our parents to be there, but the room is full of family, mostly mine, and when I walk in, the room goes quiet. "I have a son," I say, and the cheers erupt, but it's my father who catches me before I hit the floor. "I have a son," I tell him between sobs as he hugs me. "A son."

"You're going to be the best father," he says, grabbing my head and kissing me right where the cross is. "The best of the best."

"Can we see them?" Emily's mother, Dora, looks at me as she holds my mother by the shoulders, both in tears.

"Yeah, just the parents for now." I look at everyone. "Then I'll see if I can bring him out."

I'm walking with my father as my mother and Dora walk down the hallway. "Where are Kallie and Beau?" I ask, looking at them standing there hugging. "You guys," I tell them. "Come on."

"Oh, no," Kallie says, never overstepping as always. "It's good."

"Beau," I tell him, and he just nods at me and brings Kallie with him. She holds my hand, and I look down at her, the tears running down her face.

"I'm so proud of you," she says, hugging me now, and

when we walk into the room, my eyes automatically do a sweep to make sure I see both of them there.

My mother hands the baby to Dora, and then Emily looks at me almost as if she wants to sleep. "You ready, Daddy?" she says to me, and I just smile at her.

"What's the baby's name?" Dora asks. I look at Emily, and she nods her head.

"Well," I say, walking over to Dora as she hands me my son. "It gives me the greatest honor to introduce you to Gabriel McIntyre," I say, and it's my father who now has to be held up. He puts his hands in front of his mouth and sobs. I walk to him and then Kallie, who is equally sobbing. "Guys, meet your grandson Gabriel."

ONE WEEK LATER

I put the truck in park right by the curb and get out, grabbing the white papers in my hands. I walk through the grass and stop when I get to where I want to be. I look down, seeing pink flowers, and I laugh.

"We've never met," I say. "And you don't know me, but you sent me a gift on my twenty-first birthday." I swallow, holding the white papers up and then taking a lighter out and lighting them on fire. "For the longest time, I thought about the reason you sent them. I kept going over and over it in my head, and there was nothing that I could think of that would make this a good thing. Then I met my biological father, and I knew then that you did it out of spite. You did it because you are just a horrible fucking person. I don't know what you wanted to achieve with them, and I don't give a fuck. What you didn't do is you couldn't break the bond or the love that I have with my family. You rocked the foundation there for a bit, but what you weren't expecting is for us to build it back up stronger and better." I look at the sky as the papers turn to black ash. "I have a son, and I'm going to raise him the same way my father raised me. Love, respect, and dignity, something you don't know anything about. I hope you are rotting in fucking hell, old man," I say, placing the papers down in front of the tombstone that reads.

Mr. Clint Huntington
Loving husband & father

Books By Natasha Madison

Southern Wedding Series

Mine To Have

Mine To Hold

Mine To Cherish

Mine To Love

The Only One Series

Only One Kiss

Only One Chance

Only One Night

Only One Touch

Only One Regret

Only One Moment

Only One Love

Only One Forever

Southern Series

Southern Chance

Southern Comfort

Southern Storm

Southern Sunrise

Southern Heart

Southern Heat

Southern Secrets

Southern Sunshine

This Is

This Is Crazy

This Is Wild

This Is Love

This Is Forever

Hollywood Royalty

Hollywood Playboy

Hollywood Princess

Hollywood Prince

Something Series

Something So Right

Something So Perfect

Something So Irresistible

Something So Unscripted

Something So BOX SET

Tempt Series

Tempt The Boss

Tempt The Playboy

Tempt The Hookup

Heaven & Hell Series

Hell and Back

Pieces of Heaven

Heaven & Hell Box Set

Love Series

Perfect Love Story

Unexpected Love Story

Broken Love Story

Mixed Up Love

Faux Pas